Fiction
Kilgore, John, 1916-
The Sun devils

THE SUN DEVILS

Frank Walker had been eluding the vengeance-seeking Kimball brothers when the Navajo diverted him to a hidden rancheria where he was to care for a wounded white man—an outlaw with no respect for Indians. Frank had to ride hard when the Kimballs found him and this time it was more than just a manhunt. When the smoke eventually cleared two men were dead with more manhunters arriving than vultures. Frank wished he'd never ventured into Navajo country.

THE SUN DEVILS

John Kilgore

A Lythway Book
CHIVERS PRESS
BATH

Allen County Public Library
Ft. Wayne, Indiana

First published in Great Britain 1987
by
Robert Hale Limited
This Large Print edition published by
Chivers Press
by arrangement with
Robert Hale Limited
1991

ISBN 0 7451 1273 0

© Robert Hale Ltd 1987

British Library Cataloguing in Publication Data

Kilgore, John *1916–*
 The sun devils.
 I. Title
 813.54 [F]

ISBN 0-7451-1273-0

THE SUN DEVILS

CHAPTER ONE

THE EMPTY PLACE

To the faded, lean man on the muscled-up bay horse it was less the immensity, stillness and hush of the endless landscape he was studying from atop the red-earth barranca than it was the sensation of utter loneliness that impressed him.

For hundreds of miles there was no sign of life. There were high spires and coppery-tinted shiprock plateaux at far intervals, an occasional bosque of trees and intermittent fields of underbrush, usually on the east side of those cathedral spires or the fluted stone, flat-topped shiprocks, but there was no sign of inhabitants, either two or four-legged.

He twisted to consider the long-rolling gradual slope he had ridden up. Back a dozen miles or so were trees, junipers mostly, and rocks and heat, although this was not yet full summer. Forward the land seemed unable even to support junipers, and they grew where no other tree could survive.

It was a lunar landscape of emptiness, a place time had forgot. He studied the distant thin stands where trees grew, selected the one he hoped would have water near by and picked his way down off the red-earth barranca with dust-puffs rising each time the bay horse put a hoof down.

Nothing could exist in this timeless void without water, including trees. He knew from experience that underbrush and the pale buffalo grass which lived in shaded places derived liquid from dew, but trees required water. Junipers would grow where there was very little water, but the trees he had studied from the barranca were not junipers, they had leaves instead of needles, so they got water somewhere.

It was not a desert, although it looked like one. It was, the horseman thought, something left over from the time when the world had cooled, and perhaps the reason it had remained as it had always been was because it was too remote, too isolated from roads and towns, and there was nothing visible which was worth exploiting. Even the grass was frail. It was already making seed-heads. Everywhere else the grass would not be heading for another month or two.

Down upon the flat county aiming toward the trees which had seemed from the barranca to be about two miles distant, but which actually were closer to six miles, the horseman saw tiny 'runs' in the dusted-over crust of dry ground where something—he thought it might be kangaroo rats or something similar—scurried in search of seeds. He saw no larger 'sign' until he was approaching the trees, then there were unmistakable rabbit and bobcat tracks.

Overhead there was a flawless sky of pale turquoise, and the air was glass-like in quality; the horseman could make out minute details for miles.

He dismounted and led his horse the last couple of hundred yards, his holstered Colt free of its tie-down as he studied the trees and their speckled shade. Beyond stood one of those plinths of rust-coloured sandstone. It had two much smaller upthrusts on each side of it.

The bay horse picked up its gait a little, ears forward. The man trudged ahead, hat down, eyes narrowed, watching for anything—colour, shape, but above all movement.

There was none until he led the horse into the first shade and past the outermost trees, then wild pigeons by the dozen exploded in all directions. The horse sucked back, and the man's right hand dropped to his gunbutt. This was the only movement and noise either of them had heard in more than an hour. After the birds were gone the hush returned deeper than ever.

There was water. Barely enough on the surface, but evidently quite a bit below it otherwise the trees and the surprising lushness of the shallow, wide dished-out place which was green for about four or five acres would not have had such grass and undergrowth.

The horseman made a thorough exploration of this unexpected oasis, returned to off-saddle the bay horse, hobble it and drape saddlebags and booted Winchester from a low limb, then pitch his bedroll into dark grass and go to kneel where a sump-spring had created a puddle of blue-clear water not much larger than a man's hat.

He drank, shed his shirt, scrubbed off sweat and dust, then sat back on his haunches examining the little trails which came like veins from many directions to the edge of the pool. The largest tracks had been made by bobcats.

He went over to lie on his blankets for the sun to dry him, and without intending to slept until the sun was gone and shadows came downward from among the trees as well as from the distant barranca to bring premature dusk to his camp.

The bay horse had rolled, something hobbled horses could do only if they knew how to get up afterwards. His horse had been wearing hobbles in hundreds of camps over the last few years; he knew a lot about hobbles. In fact, he could move faster wearing hobbles than a man could run. He was a savvy, level-headed, completely dependable partner for the sun-browned man who owned him.

The rider went back to the sump and did his laundry, draped it to dry, and wearing only boots and hat went to the far side of the camp to study the land in all directions.

There was not enough feed in this whole country to interest cattlemen, even though it looked worth while. The lean man knew from experience that in land like this where grass was pale green rather than dark green, and where it was frail and headed-out too early, cattle walked themselves thin between mouthfuls. Any seasoned stockman would know this. Sheep did moderately well in this kind of country. Sheep and goats. But even then they had to be moved constantly.

It just was not commercially exploitable country and that suited the horseman very well. He walked back to the opposite side of the bosque and gazed into purpling shadows toward the barranca. In any country with leached ground wearing a parched crust horses left tracks a blind man could follow. Shod horses in particular.

He went back to scout for dry limbs and make a tiny cooking-fire. He was not a heavy feeder, which was just as well because saddlebags, even those big utility bags that were army issue, did not hold a lot, and his saddlebags were much smaller and held less.

He had been living off the land for a month. As he ate it occurred to him that the welcome things of life seemed always to have strings attached. This moonscape-country would provide him with shelter and isolation, which he needed, and it would also provide him with nothing larger than rabbits for food.

He rolled a smoke, allowed the tiny fire to die, went to see if his clothes had dried, and because they had not he returned to the fire and sat with a blanket around him like an old bronco Indian.

Some birds flew silently to roost in the treetops, uneasy about the man below and the faint scent of smoke but evidently unwilling to go elsewhere probably because they had always roosted in this place. But none were wild pigeons; from their sounds the horseman knew they were not edible birds, and having resolved his most pressing problem, to find safety in isolation, he had to consider the next most important thing, which was finding food. Right at this moment the prospects were not very good.

But he was a quiet, philosophical man, grey at the temples, blue-eyed with a slightly hawkish cast to his features; he was not much of a worrier. Nearing forty he had mastered the art of survival.

He looked around where the bay horse was dozing, rolled into the bedroll with the Colt six inches from his head, one boot on the opposite side standing upright with the bone handle of his boot-knife equally as available, and lay back gazing at the rash of blue-white stars.

He was tired but not especially sleepy. Over

the past month he and the bay horse had made many camps, some dry, some with water, all secluded, and had not stayed at any of them for more than one night. This camp too had tracks leading to it. What he needed was rain to obliterate his tracks. Those stars up yonder did not even have a veil over them. His guess was that this vast emptiness got rare interludes of rainfall.

Tomorrow they would take a southeasterly course, find another point of vantage and sit up there watching for rearward movement. For the last thirteen days they had seen none, but there were many graveyards with men in them who had become complacent.

Sleep arrived, a sickle moon belatedly arose, and the bay horse came out of its doze to lift its head, point ahead with its little ears, and stand perfectly still looking into the shadows at the north end of the bosque where some feathery trees like tamaracks grew.

Movement up there was followed by long periods of stillness, but the bay horse had not been attracted by movement, he had picked up a scent first, then movement. It did not panic him as the scent of a puma might have, but he did not like the scent either.

The silhouette did not make a sound as it moved among the feathery trees and halted near the front tier of them to gaze toward the dead little fire and the lumpy shape beside it.

Only once did the wraith seem interested in the bay horse, otherwise it was interested in the sleeping man. Eventually it squatted, which made it almost indistinguishable among the unkempt lower limbs of the lacy trees.

The horse lost some of his concern since the ghost appeared to pose no threat, and dropped its head to crop grass although it was already as full as a tick.

A rodent-hunting large owl swooped low near the sump-spring, this place evidently being on its nocturnal hunting itinerary, except that this time what it saw and scented caused panic, and it beat the air with frantic sweeps of powerful wings to gain altitude and flee.

The horse raised its head about a foot from the ground, grass protruding from both sides of its mouth as it looked for the wraith and could not make it out among the trees, went back to eating and put the strange 'thing' out of its mind.

Some small creatures came to drink as the night wore along. The timid ones fled from man-scent, but the bolder ones got their water, then fled.

CHAPTER TWO

ANASAZI

Dawn arrived as a two-toned mauve-red utterly silent explosion that filled the empty place from end to end, reflecting off the plinths and shiprocks in shades of old copper which scaled down to tawny tan.

The birds left at the first movement from below. The horse solemnly watched its rider dress in clean, dry clothing and hopped over where the wraith had been to sniff, then hop in a direction where the scent was not as rank to begin grazing.

The horseman propped a steel mirror and shaved at the sump, and after breakfast went to make a round of the bosque from the outside watching for anything foreign to this lonely place—and found tracks where pressed-flat grass led northward out to the hardpan earth crust and lost them, but they had seemed to have been made by someone who had approached from the east.

A good sign-reader would have read a lot more from them than Frank Walker could. His knowledge of sign was limited to tracking stray horses and cattle. Like most stockmen that had always been about the extent of his interest in tracking.

He stood in cool shadows with his back to the bosque and waited a long time, saw nothing, and in the end gave it up and returned to roll his blankets and prepare to strike camp. He liked this place, felt comfortable in it, and even liked the silence and emptiness, the haunting beauty of the dawn and the impression of timelessness that went with it. Also, whoever had scouted him up last night had not come from the north or west, which meant that they had probably seen him come down here from the barranca and had not been tracking him.

If they had tracked him down they would not have been content to satisfy their curiosity from a distance of fifty yards without moving closer. They would have walked up, put a pistol to his temple, blown his brains out, tied him belly-down across a saddle and gone back the way they had come.

As a riddle it was interesting, and perhaps as a threat it was negligible, but it had been his intention to ride on come dawn, and now he was striking camp to do this.

He brought the bay horse close in, looped and secured the hobbles, bridled the animal and smoothed out his doubled saddleblanket, raised the saddle high and eased it down, fished for the cinch, got everything ready and turned to pick up the saddlebags to tie them behind the cantle—and froze.

There were four of them standing like stone seemingly unarmed watching everything Frank Walker had been doing.

They were Indians. Well put-up men a shade over average height and not as dark as some Indians Frank had seen. Two of them wore headbands and two had braids. One man was wearing a faded red velvet shirt. The other three wore equally as faded blue cotton work-shirts.

Where they had come from Frank had no idea, but as he stood facing them he was sure of one thing: the man who had scouted up his camp last night was either one of them or had told these four about him.

He knew they were Navajos, but that was all he knew, and unless they spoke English there was not going to be much conversation because Frank Walker knew no Navajo and not enough border-Spanish to crowd on the head of a pin. He watched them. They were evidently not hasty men. Their expressions told him nothing. Finally, he took a chance and spoke to the man wearing the faded red shirt.

'Howdy.'

The Indian, who seemed younger than his companions, kept his face blank as he said, '*Yah teh.*'

Frank regarded the man; he had not answered in English, but if what he'd said in his own language was the equivalent to 'howdy' then the Navajo probably understood English; some English at any rate.

The silence grew awkward, and since it appeared the Indians were not going to break it Frank spoke directly to the younger man again. 'Something I can do for you?'

This time the reply was in English. 'Are you a doctor?'

Frank shook his head. 'No.'

The youngest man said something guttural. One of his companions spoke curtly in the same language, and the youngest Navajo said, 'You come anyway.'

Frank studied them. He did not fear them but neither did he believe mounting his horse and starting to ride away was likely to be successful. He was correct. Four additional Indians came up on horseback and sat like statues, silent and motionless. Frank nodded at the youngest man, mounted the bay horse and followed as the Indians turned eastward.

The four unmounted Navajos had horses a mile away behind a flourishing stand of thornpin brush. When they too were astride the ride was resumed. No one spoke, and only occasionally did any of the Indians look at Frank.

They had been riding for almost two hours when he eased up beside the man in the red shirt and said, 'Why do you need a doctor?'

The coppery-skinned man turned eyes the

colour of wet obsidian when he replied. 'It was my idea. I went to the Indian school four years. Our medicine is good. Your medicine is better for some things.'

Frank wagged his head. 'I told you, I'm not a doctor.'

The Navajo rode along looking ahead as though he had not heard, and Frank let go a long breath. He did not know a whole lot about redskins but what he did know included this exasperating custom of acting deaf when they wanted to.

One of the men in blue cotton drifted back, ignored Frank and spoke to his companion. The youngest Indian answered shortly, then faced Frank again. 'He wants to know why you came into our country.'

'I didn't know it was your country. It didn't look to me like it belonged to anyone. I didn't even see a coyote.'

'But you came. Why?'

Frank looked at both of them. It was like staring at two stone walls. 'Because I was heading for the border,' he said.

This was also interpreted, then the pair of Indians stared at him for a while before the older one rode ahead and the younger one, watching the older one ride away, said, 'Maybe once a year, maybe once every two or three years outlaws come down through our country trying to reach Mexico. Some of them we see but mostly they pass through in the night and we only find their tracks.' The black eyes studied Frank. 'There is an Indian Agency over that way,' he gestured in a southeasterly direction, then dropped his arm. 'Seventy miles. It has policemen, and until last year it had soldiers too.' His gaze at Frank was speculative now. 'Otherwise we never see white men. There is no reason for them to come through here; we have nothing they want. They took everything before I was born. Why are you an outlaw?'

Frank looked directly back at the Indian when he replied. 'Because I was born the same way you were—knowing right from wrong and not being able to do a hell of a lot about it.'

Whatever that enigmatic answer meant to the Indian Frank Walker would never know. At that moment one of the Indians riding ahead turned and called out to the younger Navajo who immediately kneed his horse and loped ahead leaving Frank to himself.

There was a council in progress up where the Indians were riding. Frank thought it had to do with him. They were bending northerly now riding toward a huge shiprock which arose abruptly out of the red-tan earth, its lower walls curved rock which straightened a third of the way up and resembled organ pipes.

They were heading around to the east side of the flat-topped mesa with warming sunlight in their faces hinting of heat to come when Frank faced to his left and saw trees which seemed to be growing out of the rib-like fluted rock and farther, perhaps a quarter of a mile out. It reminded him of the bosque where he had spent the night except for that huge drum-shaped mesa.

The bay horse raised its head. It had picked up the same unpleasant scent it had detected late in the previous night when it had caught sight of the shadowy apparition. Sheep. Frank smelled them too, but there was no settlement, no hogans or faggot corrals in sight.

The Indians rode in close to the base of the mesa, reached the trees and walked their horses on a loose rein as they approached the end of their journey.

Frank finally saw the faggot corrals and some sheep, not as many as he had expected judging from the smell, but he still saw no conical log-mud Navajo houses.

There were none. There was a cleft in the east wall of the towering mesa. Water flowed from back in there, right out of the heart of the rock.

Where the Indians halted and dismounted Frank could see up through the cleft. The reason there were no hogans was because these people lived in *anasazi* ruins which they had repaired to make them livable which had been built out of solid rock into the side of the mesa only the Lord knew how many hundreds of years earlier.

There were women and children, some older men as well as older women who glanced at Frank then looked away as though he did not exist. He passed within ten feet of people who seemed totally unaware of his presence. The man in the faded red velvet shirt waited until Frank came up then fell in beside him. He too looked everywhere except at Frank Walker. Frank had questions but did not ask them.

They took him to the ladder leading to a ledge where square rooms built around and atop each other all looked alike. Only two Indians climbed to the ledge with Frank. One was the younger man, the other was the older, weathered Indian with the stern expression, broad, thin-lipped uncompromising mouth who had ridden part way with Frank. The older man stepped away and jutted his jaw toward a doorless opening with cool dimness beyond. Frank ducked his head to enter, then straightened up. For a minute his eyes could see nothing. Gradually as they adjusted Frank saw a fat Indian woman wearing at least six turquoise necklaces sitting on the ground beside a rush pallet. The room was blessedly cool. It smelled of fresh-cut grass which Frank guessed was the result of the rush pallet having recently been renewed.

A man lying on his side facing away from

Frank was on the pallet. There was a clay water-jug and two clay plates beside the pallet.

Frank glanced over his shoulder. The Indians who had escorted him were looking in. They were staring at the man on the pallet and did not look at Frank until he blew out a rough breath and approached the pallet. Immediately the large woman arose and swept out of the room making scarcely a sound.

Frank knelt, then looked back. 'I told you; I am not a doctor.' Neither Indian appeared to have heard, they were still staring at the prone man.

Frank said, 'Hell; I don't know what to do for sick people,' and reached to ease the prone man over onto his back. Two light blue eyes looked straight up at him from a beard-stubbled, haggard face. The man's lips were cracked and swollen, his body sagged inward at the middle, but the look in his eyes was perfectly rational. He was a white man.

Frank's shock held him motionless for a moment. He looked down, saw the caked dark red crust on the man's upper trouser-leg, leaned slightly for a better look, then slowly pulled back to meet the pale eyes again. Whoever he was he had been shot. From his general appearance he had been shot and left to die somewhere. His soiled clothing hung on a frame which normally would have been heavy and powerful.

He had cracked, swollen lips from thirst. Frank rocked back and said, 'Mister, you look like hell.'

The pale eyes neither blinked nor glowed. They remained fixed on Frank's face with a gunmetal dullness. The cracked lips opened slightly as the wounded man forced words out.

'The bullet—cut it out. These people—don't cut they pray and sprinkle pollen or something. Dig it out.'

Frank motioned for the men in the doorway to get out of the light then bent over to make a close examination of the wound. The trouser-leg had been slit. The leg itself was grotesquely swollen. He raised it and heard the man's teeth grinding from agony. He raised it higher then gently put it down again.

'There's no bullet in your leg,' he told the pale-eyed man whose face was now drenched with sweat. 'The bone isn't even broken. Nicked maybe, but the bullet went to the outside of your leg. It made a mess coming out in back. How long ago did this happen? You got caked blood all over. You must have bled like a stuck hawg. How long ago?'

The man gazed steadily up at Frank Walker without parting his lips, and gradually slipped into unconsciousness. His breathing was not shallow but it was fluttery.

Frank stood up, winced when one knee shot pain, and went back out into the increasing heat. Down below at least fifteen people were working. Children played. Beyond the secret cleft he could see to a horizon that reached so far it began to curve before a bluish haze obscured it.

He looked at the Navajo who had been to one of the Indian schools—they were taken from their parents as small children and kept at those schools until they finished high school, allowed only rare visits home.

'Who is he? What's he doing here? What happened to him?'

The Navajo peeked into the room as he answered. 'Children out with the sheep found him. He was just like you see him. Maybe he was lyin' out there close to a week. He had a carbine, his pistol, and an old saddlebag, that was all. We did not track his horse. After that long it would be a long ways from here. We don't know what happened; he was not shot near here. The sound of a gunshot travels many miles in this air. No one heard a gunshot. We brought him here because he would have been dead in another day lying out there in the sun without water. He has never talked except when he was out of his head. The woman who takes care of him does not talk English. He's never said anything when I've been in the room with him. We don't know who he is, but—' The younger man glanced past at the grim-faced older man. He spoke curtly. The older man turned without answering, led the way to the adjoining little cube-like mud room and ducked to enter. In the middle of this room which had no furniture was a single saddlebag, obviously one of a pair.

The older Navajo jutted his jaw and said something brusque which Frank interpreted to mean that he was to examine the single saddlebag.

It was stuffed with paper bills of fairly large denomination. Frank pulled some of it out and held it to the light, then began counting. He gave up when he reached seven thousand dollars, and that was only the value of the greenbacks he'd taken from the saddlebag; it had easily two or three times that much money still in it.

He stolidly punched all the money back inside the bag, buckled the strap and got to his feet, looking at the Indians. He said, 'Water.'

They took him down off the ledge to the icy spring, and after he had tanked up he removed his hat to mop off sweat, and eyed them. They gazed steadily back. He instinctively knew that the older man had never seen a steam locomotive, heard a telegraph key, seen himself in a glass mirror or eaten with a fork, but he knew the man with the bullet-hole in him had stolen that money.

He sat down on a rock to wipe his hatband before putting the hat on. He fished for his makings and rolled a smoke, lit it and with smoke drifting he looked at the pair of Indians. 'I can't do anything for him your woman can't do. Maybe not as much. His leg looks like hell, but it seems to be if he'd been going to catch the gangrene it would have showed up by now and his leg would look like rotten meat.'

They listened without taking their eyes off him, but made no comment, so he stood up as he said, 'What do you expect me to do?'

The younger Navajo answered promptly. 'Take care of him. He is a white man. We will bring food, but he is a white man. You take care of him.'

CHAPTER THREE

DOUBTS

Frank smoked and thought, stubbed out the quirley, eyed his companions, then shrugged and nodded. His reason for agreeing to tend the injured man had nothing to do with compassion. Frank was a realistic individual; no one would ever find him in this secret canyon on the east side of the big mesa. He needed rest, so did his bay horse. He drank more cold water then stood up facing the man in the faded red velvet shirt. 'What's your name?' he asked.

'At the school they gave me the name of Charley. That man is my grandfather, his name is Begay. You call him Hosteen. What is your name?'

'Frank.'

'That's all?'

'Yes, that's all. Charley, are you the only one among these folks who can speak English?'

Charley glanced down the broad cleft where people were busy before replying. 'No, others, were also taken to the school. But they don't want to talk in English.' Charley looked back at Frank. 'Can you talk Spanish?'

'No. I'd starve in Spanish. How about Hosteen; does he know what I'm saying?'

'No. But he can speak a little Spanish. Most Navajos know some Spanish.'

'Charley, suppose someone came riding from the west.'

The Navajo's black eyes glinted. 'What would they see? Same thing you saw. Nothing.'

'I'm not talkin' about greenhorns, Charley, I'm talkin' about trackers.'

The older man broke in with a guttural harangue. Charley answered, and the old buck gazed at Frank for a moment then said something in a dry tone of voice and Charley laughed. 'My grandfather said there will be no tracks for anyone to see. He said the people go so far even the Sun Devils can't find them but damned white men come anyway.'

Frank considered the old man, read veiled hostility in the set of his wide, lipless mouth and turned back toward the younger man. 'Brushing out my tracks won't fool them. They'll scout.'

Charley shook his head. 'They won't find you. At a council last week one of the speakers said other white men will be looking for that wounded man. We went back and brushed out his sign too.'

Frank turned that over in his mind. He had not considered this other possibility, he'd thought only of his own danger, but now he toted up the odds and did not like them. He was satisfied the other white man was also an outlaw. If possemen were scouting for him too, regardless of what the Navajos thought, sooner or later trouble would find this hidden place.

Charley cut across Frank's thoughts. 'They may come here to our rancheria but there will be no sign of white men.'

Frank was not entirely reassured. He did not know Indians but he did know white men. He blew out a big breath, looked down the shaded, grassy canyon which widened where it ended at the base of the mesa, and made his decision. He would stay, but only until instinct told him it was no longer safe to do so.

'I'll care for my horse and fetch my outfit up to that room where the wounded man is. Charley, at the first hint of riders you come let me know.'

They went down with him and helped haul his outfit to the little room. The heat was noticeable out away from the shiprock-mesa beyond the final stand of trees. Elsewhere, though, it was much cooler, and in the little dark room where Frank and the Navajos dumped his belongings it was even cooler. It was also shadowy because the only opening was the doorway and it faced northeast and did not catch the first sun rays.

The fat woman brought food and another earthen pot of water. She did not look at Frank and padded away as silently as she had arrived.

He took his bedroll to the far side of the room and unrolled it, then went over beside the wounded man. He was sleeping. His breathing was close to normal, there was sweat on his face despite the coolness, and beneath the sun-bronzed skin of his face there was an unhealthy pallor.

Frank, who was a confirmed believer in the medicinal value of whisky, stood looking down and wishing he had a bottle. He knelt, rolled up his sleeves, washed his hands then went to work washing the wounded man's terribly swollen leg.

The man awakened. Frank went on cleaning the wound as he said, 'It don't smell so I guess it's not infected. You're damned lucky. Why didn't they take the money when they shot you?'

Instead of replying to the question the wounded man said, 'You got to be a blacksmith. No one could be that rough and clumsy otherwise. Who the hell are you an' where'd you come from?'

Frank rocked back and grinned. 'Partner, all I know about bad wounds is that they got to be kept clean, the flies got to be kept away from them, and since I didn't ask for this job but got it anyway, if you don't like the way I do things you can suck eggs. Why didn't they take the money?'

The wounded man's head sank back, sweat covered his face and he locked his jaws against the pain. The swollen leg was so sore that just fingertip-pressure caused him agony. His eyes were closed when he spoke through gritted teeth. 'Where the hell is this place?'

'Up a split in the mesa hidden by trees for a quarter mile eastward and you couldn't find it with both hands unless you smelled the goats and sheep.'

'How long have I been here?'

'I don't know; maybe a week. They are Navajos.'

'I know that, damn it. Who are you?'

'Name is Frank. I just came riding along.'

The blue eyes opened. 'No one just comes ridin' along into country like this. A man could die out there and his clothes'd be out of style before anyone found his carcass. I covered at least thirty miles. I outdistanced them. Where's my horse? He's a thoroughbred; I gave six hundred dollars for him down in the Eagle Pass country.'

Frank finished with the leg and propped the outlaw up so he could drink from one of the water-pots. Afterwards he roughly hauled the outlaw back so he could sit up, propped against the rough mud wall. He squatted in front of the propped-up man. 'Your horse ran off an' the Indians brushed out your tracks. What's your name?'

'Smith.'

Frank grinned. 'What's your first name, Mister Smith—John?'

'Yeah, John.'

'Why didn't they take the money?'

'Because, you nosy bastard, they couldn't keep up. I told you I outrun them. I came at least thirty miles into the most desolate, empty, unfriendly country I ever saw, and somewhere back yonder they turned back. That much I remember. I don't think they knew they shot me. Everyone was shooting. I don't have no recollection of fallin' off the horse.'

'John, somethin' is bothering me. They were after you like the devil after a crippled saint; they knew you had the money, and that was more'n a week ago and you left tracks heading up into this country. Where are those men now?'

John stared a long time at Frank without speaking. 'They give it up, maybe. Would you risk dyin' of thirst trying to find someone who was one full day ahead, so far ahead you couldn't even see him, in country like this?'

Frank wagged his head. 'John, you're either a fool or bein' sick's upset your brain. I told you—your horse ran off after you hit the ground. They'd find him sure as gawd made little green apples, and they'd see the blood an' know you were out here somewhere, on foot, wounded bad. There's an awful lot of money in that saddlebag. The world is full of men who'd risk thirst or anything else to get their paws on your saddlebag. John, they're out there as sure as we're sitting here.'

The pale-eyed man said, 'Do you know what *pulque* is?'

'No.'

'It's whisky made from fermented desert plants. Messicans live on the stuff. Navajos make it too. See if you can find us some.'

Frank rolled a smoke, lit it and continued to hunker in the blessed coolness, eyeing John Smith. At one time Smith had been a large, muscular man. He still had the testy gaze of someone who would put up a battle without much encouragement. Frank guessed Smith to be about Frank's age, or perhaps a year or two older. Instead of going in search of Indian whisky Frank said, 'Where are your guns?'

Smith looked around as though he had not missed them before. 'They took 'em, I guess. Why? You figuring on making a run for it with my money, you—'

'John, you got mouth trouble. The next time you call me a name, bad leg or no bad leg, I'm going to break your jaw. I hadn't thought about running off with your saddlebag, but it's not a bad idea—except that the more I think about this mess the more I believe neither one of us could go ten miles before we'd be scouted up. Tell me something, John. Where did you get that money?'

Smith was deeply inhaling second-hand cigarette smoke. Frank handed him what remained of the quirley then waited for the answer that did not come. Smith smoked and stared at Frank, and remained silent.

Charley came to the doorway to glance in. Frank arose and walked out along the ledge toward the adjoining little room, but he did not enter, he instead leaned against the ancient mud wall gazing thoughtfully down the beautiful wide and cool arroyo. Whatever a man had done it didn't seem he deserved to be stuck in a country that looked like the backsides of the moon with the only other white man in God knew how many miles, who was a surly son of a bitch.

Charley said, 'He looks better,' and Frank

Walker put a wry look upon the Navajo. 'I'm not so sure you folks shouldn't have buried him out there, Charley.' The Indian also leaned against the cool old mud wall, looking down the canyon.

'They're looking for him,' Frank said. 'Yeah, I know; Indians know all about hiding tracks. I know somethin' else too; Hosteen said white men come anyway. He was right. There is one hell of a lot of money behind us. I can feel it in my bones; they're goin' to find him. They got his horse by now sure as hell. They know he's hurt and they know he's on foot. Charley, they aren't going to give up.'

The Indian picked a hungry woodtick off his sleeve and killed it between his thumbnails. 'They won't find him or you if they find this place,' he said. 'There is nothing to show you two are with the people.'

Frank thought about that too. There were enough Indian men to prevent possemen, or whoever was searching for John Smith, from forcing their way up in here to make a search, but all that meant was that the possemen would go seventy miles back and return with Indian policemen or maybe even the army. He sighed. 'I think maybe your grandfather is right: white men bring trouble.'

Charley looked at Frank, who was gazing out where his horse was placidly grazing among the Indian animals. From what he had seen his bay horse was the only shod animal at the rancheria. Maybe the Indians would overlook this, but possemen wouldn't. Charley said, 'A Roadman is coming tomorrow.'

The statement was made casually as though Frank would know what it meant, but he did not know. 'What the hell is a Roadman, Charley?'

'Navajo healer—preacher. He was sent for because there is going to be a marriage. The people have to pay; if they pay enough he will make a ceremony that lasts seven days, all night and all day.'

Frank was eyeing the Indian with perplexity. 'What's this Roadman got to do with me and what's-his-name in there with the gunshot wound?'

'Roadmen visit all the rancherias and settlements. They know all the news. He will know something about the wounded man. Maybe he will know something about you.'

Frank returned to gazing out where the horses were. He said, 'You got any shoe pullers—tongs—something I can use to pull the shoes off my horse?' At the blank look he got he said, 'Charley, Indians don't shoe their horses, white men do shoe their horses. Anyone who rides in here is goin' to see shod-horse tracks among the barefoot-horse tracks. You understand?'

Instead of answering Charley turned to lead

the way over to the ladder and down off the ledge. He stopped near a stone hut of great age built at ground level in the meadow, ducked to enter and emerged moments later with an ancient pair of the kind of tongs used by blacksmiths for lifting cherry-red steel from forge fires.

Frank took them and grimaced; pulling shoes with those tongs wouldn't be much better than pulling them by hand. It could be done though, so he and Charley went out to catch the bay horse.

Frank swore each time the tongs lost their grip, but he persevered until all four shoes had been pulled, then he tossed them behind some rocks in tall grass and handed back the tongs. His shirt was drenched with perspiration even though he had been working in tree-shade. Charley read Frank's expression correctly and grinned.

'You need water,' he said.

Frank squinted. *'Pulque.'*

Charley shook his head. 'No *pulque*. My grandfather won't allow it.'

'Is your grandfather head man?'

'We are all related. My grandfather took over when my grandmother died. She was head of this family of the people.' At Frank's puzzled expression Charley explained a little more fully. 'The women own everything, except maybe a man's guns or saddle and other little things.

They own the sheep, the goats, the horses. When a Navajo marries he is supposed to take his wife's name; the children are hers. He is supposed to move in with her clan among the people.'

Frank turned to watch his horse go back among the other horses to graze. He really was on the backside of the moon. 'Water then,' he muttered and led off in the direction of the spring.

Charley walked behind Frank with an amused twinkle in his black eyes.

CHAPTER FOUR

PLANS

John Smith accepted the lack of *pulque* with the same sour expression he showed after Frank had cleaned and replaced the bandaging on his injured leg and made a cheerful commentary.

'It's looking better. You're going to have one hell of a scar on the back of your leg, but it's healing. You owe these folks, John.'

'Stole my damned horse,' Smith snarled. 'They'll most likely steal everythin' else before I can get up and—'

'They didn't steal your horse. There's no thoroughbred among their animals,' exclaimed

Frank, getting to his feet. 'But I'll tell you something, partner; if you still had the horse you'd owe them him an' a lot more for saving your life.'

Smith raised his eyes. 'Fetch my saddlebag in here where I can keep an eye on it.'

Frank went next door and returned with the saddlebag. Smith opened the flap and felt through the money, then rebuckled the flap and put a mean look on Frank. 'Maybe the In'ians got no use for my money, but you sure as hell have.'

Frank sighed and shifted his weight to stand hipshot with his right hand on the butt of his holstered Colt. 'If I'd wanted to steal your money I could have done it—I could still do it. You couldn't stop me, John.'

'Where are my guns?'

'I don't know. I guess the Indians have them.'

'I want them.'

Frank shook his head. 'Not if I got anything to say about it.'

Smith held the saddlebag in his lap with both hands. 'You're after it,' he stated, and Frank stood looking down into the unshaven, peeling face of the other man, wondering for the second time why in all this enormous expanse of timeless land he had to fetch up in the company of this kind of a son of a bitch.

The hefty woman with six necklaces padded

into the room with two clay plates, put them down without glancing at either man and padded back out of the room. Smith looked at the plates and said, 'Goat meat or gummer mutton. And ground corn. There are antelope in this damned country; anything is better'n stinkin' mutton and goat meat that the longer you chew it the bigger it gets.' He raised his pale eyes again. 'You know anything about Navajos?'

Frank answered shortly. 'Nope. I'm not from down in this country.'

The pale blue eyes grew speculative. 'Where are you from then?'

Frank made a crooked, mirthless smile. 'None of your damned business. Anythin' else you want to know?'

Smith reached for one of the plates, ignoring Frank.

Frank took the other plate to the far side of the room and sat on his bedroll as he ate. Smith was right; goat meat was tougher than whang leather and the Navajos put some kind of hot sauce in the corn, but anything beat a dirt pile.

By the time he was ready to bed down the fat woman had come for their empty plates, and this time she looked squarely at Frank and smiled. It was so unexpected he forgot to smile back.

Charley brought a candle to replace the burned-down one on the dish near John Smith's pallet. He handed Frank a small round stone and grinned from ear to ear.

Frank examined the stone, then rolled it between his fingers. In a dubious tone he said, 'Thanks. What's it for?'

'When a Navajo girl likes a man she throws little rocks at him.'

Frank stopped rolling the rock and raised his eyes to the grinning Indian. 'Wait a minute. *Her*?'

'She is my aunt. She owns sixty ewes and four horses. She can make yucca soap and weave better than anyone else. Her husband died seven years ago. She is the one who is going to pay the Roadman for his seven-day ceremony.'

From accumulating shadows upon the far side of the room came a raucous, derisive burst of laughter. With dusk darkening everything it was difficult to see John Smith, but Frank looked in his direction anyway. While glaring over there he addressed the young Indian. 'Charley, does she know how to put poison in food?'

After Charley left and John Smith settled painfully for the night Frank took both their supper plates outside and put them near the door for the woman with sixty ewes and four horses to gather up without having to come into the room to do it.

Some time during the late night he heard

coyotes. They were close enough to awaken him, probably drawn that close by the smell of sheep.

He went outside in his stocking-feet to have a smoke and take the measure of the night. There was a three-quarter moon which made soft light among the trees and above the open grassy places, otherwise the timeless land lay hushed and unchanged from the Beginning. He killed the smoke, listened to the foraging coyotes moving off toward the far side of the mesa, and saw three Indians padding back through the trees carrying Winchesters. Without ever having been involved with sheep he knew that the bane of those who had were coyotes; they would sneak into a corral, start sheep running, then for sport race in beside them and tear out their throats.

Evidently the armed Indians had sent the coyotes off on a different course tonight.

A tall shape emerged from the shadows and stopped near by, spoke gutturally and waited for an answer which Frank could not give. He spoke back in English. 'I guess so—whatever you said, Hosteen.'

The old man with the hawk-like forbidding features spoke again, 'You think they will come.' It was a statement not a question, but Frank gazed at the old man not because of what he had said but because he had said it in English. Charley had said his grandfather did not know any English. Presumably a grandson would know his grandfather all his life. Frank wagged his head at the old man. 'Yeah, I think they will come, and so do you.'

Hosteen turned to gaze down across the eerily beautiful canyon. He remained silent until Frank spoke again. 'Let them have the money. Most likely it belongs to them anyway.'

Hosteen turned back. 'And the man?'

Frank looked steadily back at the old Indian. 'If you don't, they'll be back with more men; maybe with soldiers draggin' a damned cannon. You'll lose people in a fight. If I know the army you'll lose a hell of a lot more—this place for instance. Hosteen, I don't give a damn what you do. I just don't like to see people who did a decent thing get punished for it. Good night.'

He returned to his bedroll more awake now than before the coyotes had arrived. Through the darkness upon the opposite side of the room John Smith was softly and wetly snoring.

Frank rolled his back to Smith and went to sleep. Hours later he awakened, grinning; the old man had been listening to people using English, maybe most of his life. It was probably his dislike of white people that would not allow him to use their language—and the damned old fraud had no doubt implied wisdom about the behaviour of white people among his clansmen, even his closest relations, by pretending he did not understand English.

John Smith's leg was less swollen this morning, but if there was less pain it did not seem to improve his disposition; maybe nothing would do that. He snarled as Frank worked on his wound.

Frank ignored the ingratitude because he was becoming accustomed to it. He left the room as the sun arrived, went down to the spring to wash, and afterwards went out to see how his horse was making out.

Several people were lining out sheep for the adolescent herders who would take them out in search of browse. The children were cheerful and gabbled like small geese. They had dogs with them, but for some reason the Navajos did not train dogs to be used with sheep; their sole reason for going with the herders seemed to be to provide companionship and to warn of coyotes.

Charley came through the trees to grunt his usual greeting in Navajo and walk past to help with the sheep. Frank ambled eastward out through the trees to watch sunrise come to the stark, empty miles. What stuck in a man's craw in this country was the immensity of it and the death-like everlasting silence. Sounds of youthful drovers and bleating sheep did not seem to impinge. In fact, all sound appeared to ride across the wall of silence like wind across a big glass window; it never penetrated nor lasted for more than moments.

Somewhere southeasterly was that settlement Charley had mentioned, but seventy miles was a two-day ride; from this particular place it might as well have been a thousand miles. Unless it was known where a rancheria was in this vast sameness searchers could criss-cross for months without success.

He watched the goats take the lead of the sheep, marching out of the trees into the sun-clear open land, watched the children and their dogs walking with the animals, and had an unsettling thought. Searchers would find grazing bands of sheep.

He leaned against a tree watching the bands split off, each band under its particular herders. He could feel trouble in his bones. Regardless of the timelessness and the orderly peacefulness of this hidden place the Indians had locked themselves into a bad situation. If they would hand over Smith and his saddlebag they could conceivably come out of this mess with little injury.

He doubted that they would hand him over, so as he turned to stroll back and caught sight of his horse dozing in chilly tree-shade it occurred to him that the best course for Frank Walker to follow was mount up and get the hell away from these people—get far away from them. He stopped to watch the horse, and to wish now he had given more thought to his situation before he'd pulled those shoes. In country like this where every step was through crusted dust as fine as flour which consisted of infinitely small pieces of abrasive rock, an unshod horse would be sore-footed within two or three days, especially one that was accustomed to being shod.

He went back near the high-standing wall of the shiprock-mesa and looked along the ledge. The fat woman was not in sight. She had probably been to the room with their food and had departed. He started up the ladder.

No one came to the room this morning. He exchanged a grunt with John Smith and leaned in the doorway wondering if there were more of these surprisingly beautiful, watered and shaded secret places in this country; wondered how many men had ridden past this one without even suspecting that just about everything people required to sustain themselves was back up in here.

Smith spoke from back in the gloom. 'You're one of two things—a fugitive or someone looking for a fugitive.'

Frank slowly turned to gaze at the other man. He did not speak until Smith had also said, 'Was you out among the horses?'

'Yeah, and if you're worrying about a big thoroughbred, forget it; there's nothing out there but broomtails and one or two worthwhile horses, including mine.'

The shadowy face held steadily in Frank's

direction. 'I can ride.'

Frank shook his head. 'Maybe a mile,' he said, and sauntered over beside the rush pallet. 'I have a feeling they're coming for you—and they'll get you.'

Smith's lipless mouth pulled flat. 'With your help. What'd you do, bring someone to the settlement? Mister, anyone likely to come here for me is goin' to catch you too.'

Frank conceded that. 'Yeah, most likely. Unless I ride away from here soon.'

John Smith continued to watch the other rangeman's face over a short interval of silence, then he said, 'Five hundred dollars if you'll help me get away from this place.'

Frank did not even consider it. 'I told you—you couldn't sit a saddle for a mile. Even if you could, where would we go? As far as a man can see there is nothing. If someone didn't run us down by tracks we'd most likely end up dried out like prunes and dead of thirst.'

Smith snorted. 'I know waterholes in this country. Maybe not this far north in it, but I know where we could reach good water in about a day's ride.'

'You couldn't stay atop a horse for a day,' Frank told the other outlaw. 'An' I got hunch that about the time we rode up to some waterhole there'd be possemen waiting. In this kind of country a bull don't have to walk fifty yards to breed all the cows he wants to breed;

all the cows got to come to a waterhole at least once every day. That'd apply to possemen too; they just got to sit and wait.'

John Smith started to say something ugly, but a thick shadow at the doorway distracted him. The large lady with all those sheep and four horses brought in food and water, put it down, straightened up facing Frank, and stood immutably looking at him. He could feel heat coming from beneath his shirt-collar.

He made a sickly smile. She seemed satisfied with that and left the room. John Smith, who had noticed nothing was already eating when Frank said, 'I'll tell you what I think, cowboy. When they ride in here, hand over that saddlebag, and maybe they'll ride away. Maybe. Maybe they'll kill you; I don't know what you did. But if you make a fight out of it they're going to get the saddlebag *and* kill you.'

Smith stopped between mouthfuls to stare upwards. 'These In'ians wouldn't let someone ride in here.'

Frank's reply to that was curt. 'I think you're right. But I'm not an Indian. I don't much like the idea of you using these people to hide behind.' Frank turned and reached the doorway before Smith snarled at him.

'I knew you was treacherous the moment I set eyes on you. Let me tell you something. Not you nor anyone else is goin' to hand me over—if they come—and I don't think they'll even be close by the time I'm ready to ride out of this place.'

Frank stepped out into the warming new day, saw Indian women working wet ash into stretched hides, saw other women at little beehive mud ovens, and also saw a gathering of Indian men in a small grove of trees evidently holding a council. He started down the ladder in the direction of the seated men.

CHAPTER FIVE

THE COUNCIL

There were seven Navajos sitting in the shade, and as Frank approached their black eyes turned upon him and their conversation ended. The only two he knew were Charley and his grandfather, but he thought he had seen the other men around the rancheria.

Feeling like an intruder Frank remained standing when he said, 'That man in the room with the hurt leg is coming along. The swelling is going down, the wound is healing over. I don't know a lot about wounds; I think maybe when he's all healed he'll walk with a limp, but he's doing right well and don't need me any more.'

Charley, who had been listening to each

word, continued to stare upwards at Frank Walker after silence came. For a long time he did not move, then eventually he interpreted for the other Indians, and after he had done that they too sat like stones through a prolonged interval of silence. When Frank had about decided none of them were going to speak, Hosteen said something brusque, and Charley raised obsidian eyes to Frank again. 'This here is Moses Dominguez—the Roadman. He came in just ahead of sunrise.'

Frank flicked a glance at the lined, bird-like Indian who was watching him with eyes like a ferret, black and intense. He had no idea what a Navajo healer or preacher or whatever Moses Dominguez was should look like; to Frank he looked like any other wizened, lined old Navajo buck.

Charley leaned forward slightly from the waist. 'He saw sun devils at sunrise.'

The way Charley said this implied something serious, but since Frank had no idea what a sun devil was he could only show Charley a puzzled expression.

Charley did not explain, he said instead that if Frank intended to leave the rancheria it was too late for him to do it, and that implication was understandable enough. Frank said, 'Why?'

Charley glanced at the Roadman, who spoke in a slightly rough tone of voice as though he had throat trouble. Charley looked up again. 'He says the sun devils were moving north; he also said they would cross his tracks and he knows they would have someone go looking for him or for where he was going.'

Frank was tired of standing, and although he suspected he was not supposed to sit down unless invited to do so, he sank to his haunches as he said, 'What the hell is a sun devil?'

Charley had demonstrated that he had humour. Now he showed a faint twinkle but otherwise remained expressionless as he replied. 'A reflection. The people know not to wear shiny things. Bits are made to rust, gun barrels are sometimes browned in fire, goat bells are browned too, silver is not burnished. Sun devils usually mean enemies. In the history of the people soldiers had sun devils that bounced off sword cases and buckles and gun barrels. Mexicans had even more sun devils because they wore lots of silver and liked to shine it.'

Frank nodded comprehension. 'All right. I understand. What about the sun devils the Roadman saw?'

Charley jutted his jaw. 'Coming up from the south. That's mostly what we been talking about. From what the Roadman said we think they are following the far-away tracks of the wounded man.'

Hosteen said something, and Charley interpreted it. 'We sent two men to spy. So far they have not come back. We think when they come back they will tell us it is a band of armed policemen or possemen.'

Frank got more comfortable, looked around, wagged his head in Charley's direction and said, 'If they're coming from the south and they're not in sight yet, Charley, I can saddle up and ride northwest keepin' the big mesa between me and them and they won't see me. Maybe later they'll pick up my tracks but by then it might be night again—and I don't figure to stop all night.'

Charley turned this into Navajo. The council members sat looking at the ground for a long time, then Hosteen spoke and his grandson interpreted for Frank's benefit. 'You can't ride in that direction.'

'Why not?'

'Because there are four riders over there on the barranca where your tracks end. They have been over there since yesterday. The minute they see a rider out here they will come down off the barranca.' Charley paused before also saying, 'One of them is a big man wearing a badge.'

Frank's face darkened. 'Why didn't you tell me this yesterday?'

'Because there was nothing to tell except that they were up there. They don't know what to do; they are still up there. If they knew what to do they would be doing it, instead they are just up there making a camp. There will be nothing to tell you until they do something.'

Frank spat aside and ran a slow, annoyed look around among the Indians. No wonder these people had been overrun by most of their enemies; they sat in tree-shade discussing abstractions when they should have been either fleeing like hell or riding forth to fight.

Well, he was boxed in. Maybe the intentions of the Navajo had been good, but sure as hell the results of their good intentions weren't good. Not only that, but if the men who had been stopped for lack of Frank's tracks across the immense wasteland were still up there on that damned barranca frustrated and getting meaner by the hour, if they caught sight of other white men coming up-country they'd ride down and join up with them, and that, Frank thought, would settle everyone's hash.

And he had learned something this morning. If Indians thought reflected sunlight off shiny bits and spurs and whatnot were ill omens—'sun devils'—those riders on the barranca would see the reflections from the other possemen, or whoever in hell they were, and would use them to locate the second band of horsemen, which meant that the sun devils would be worse for Frank Walker than they probably would be for the Navajos.

Hosteen's black eyes were fixed on Frank like the eyes of a rattlesnake. The other Indians studied their moccasins, the ground, their hands and only occasionally looked at the white man.

Frank shoved his hat back, eyed the old man bleakly and spoke directly to him in English. 'All right, gents. I don't know whether I can do it, but I'm goin' to make a run of it—eastward. You tell me where there's water out there and I'll take some of those sons of bitches away from your camp.' He paused, still returning old Hosteen's stare. 'They'll know I been here, so some of 'em'll come here to give you hell for puttin' me up. It'll be up to you what you tell them. I got a hunch they're not going to be happy about me being here, and if they find John Smith in your case, they're not goin' to be pleasant about that either.'

Frank arose and reset his hat. He knew he should thank them for harbouring him even though they had only done it because they had not wanted John Smith to die in their rancheria. He forced himself to gruffly mention his gratitude, then he said, 'Where is water east of here?' and pointed with an upraised arm to be certain they understood the direction he intended to take.

Old Hosteen rocked back and gazed at his grandson, but before he could request an interpretation the Roadman offered one in his thready voice, which made Frank look sardonically at the older man; he did not need an interpretation any more than Frank needed a third leg, the damned old fraud. Still, he would keep the old man's secret.

When the translation had been made Hosteen swung his gaze toward his grandson to reply shortly, and Charley looked at Frank. 'You stay. It wouldn't make any difference; we could tell you where to find the water; it wouldn't make any difference because they could run you down over there too, so you stay.'

Frank stared. 'Do you know what'll happen if they find two outlaws in your camp?'

Charley smiled. 'We are dumb Indians. We found a hurt man and another white man rode in. That's all Indians know. We tried to help the hurt white man.'

Frank swore under his breath, then checked his exasperation when he replied to Charley. 'All right, you're dumb Indians; maybe because they'll believe the hurt white man was taken in because of your kindness might help you. Charley—where does that leave me? I'm not goin' to sit here under a damned tree and let them ride up and aim guns at me.'

Charley's smile did not fade. 'They won't find you.' He raised an arm to point northward beyond the rancheria. 'They may find shod-horse tracks going that way. For many miles.' He lowered his arm, still smiling up at Frank. 'You thought we were dumb about your shod horse. A man rode your horse a long ways before you pulled his shoes, and brought him back dragging two blankets.' Charley's smile broadened. 'They won't find you here. There is a place they can't find you.'

The longer Frank stood in silence gazing at Charley the more the older men lost interest in the ground and their feet and looked up at the white man's expression. None of them smiled, but Frank had a feeling that they were laughing at him.

They could have done what Charley had just explained. He'd been busy with John Smith and settling in most of his first day at their camp. Why in hell hadn't they told him they'd laid a false trail? He wagged his head at them. He was learning something about Navajos: they did things, then they sat in shade discussing what they had done, not, as Frank had thought, to consider what should be done. It had already been done.

Old Hosteen's black gaze was bright with something close to bleak amusement—or perhaps Indian triumph. Frank fished around for his depleted makings and rolled a smoke under their poker-faced looks, lighted it and blew a pale cloud, then said, 'John Smith?'

Hosteen spoke to his grandson, and Charley interpreted for him, overlooking the way the old man had given an answer in Navajo before anyone had translated from Frank to him.

'That's what we been talking about. We

would give the saddlebag full of money to them—but would they believe we found it and didn't find the hurt man?'

Frank shook his head. 'Not on your life they wouldn't. Even if he hadn't been wounded they'll know he couldn't have escaped you fellers because he was on foot. Look at that country out there; a bug couldn't move over it without being seen.'

'My grandfather says we can show them a fresh grave. A week before you came an old man died. We buried him around the mesa.'

Frank inhaled, exhaled, and looked at the seated men. Maybe it would work. Even if those possemen had digging tools which was unlikely or if they borrowed such tools from the Indians, no one really felt good about opening a fresh grave. He shrugged, and instead of agreeing that Hosteen's ruse might work he said, 'Charley, you folks are gettin' in a little deeper by the hour.' He ranged a look around and let his gaze come to rest on Hosteen before speaking further. 'You got a hell of a lot to lose and not a damned thing to gain by buying into my troubles and John Smith's troubles. If those sons of bitches suspect you're hiding us—' Frank did not finish it, he continued to stare at old Hosteen, and balefully shook his head.

Hosteen looked at the wizened Indian with the grainy voice, and the Roadman spoke sharply, using his hands like a Mexican to gesture with.

Not another word was said to Frank Walker as the council members arose and walked away through the trees with their backs to Frank. Only Charley remained, and he was not at all talkative as he watched the older men depart, but eventually he turned, eyeing the white man, and jerked his head for Frank to follow him.

Frank expected to be led to the secret place the Indians had indicated they would hide him; instead they returned to the ladder and climbed to the ledge, then entered the little cool, gloomy room where John Smith was dozing, having eaten his food as well as the food left for Frank by the woman with sixty ewes and four horses.

Charley halted beside the rush pallet gazing stonily downward. Frank stepped closer for a look at the sleeping man's injured leg. More swelling had gone; the actual bullet-hole in front had not bled through the bandage. Smith was recovering fast, now that he'd been able to lie in a cool, shadowy place and be fed well with nothing else to do but rest since they had brought him here.

Frank stepped back to say, 'He's goin' to be awkward to move.'

Charley did not seem to consider moving Smith much of a problem. He jutted his chin. 'Where is the saddlebag?'

'Under him, I guess.'

'He don't look very heavy. You and I can get

him over to the ladder. Others will help get him down to the ground from there.'

Smith's eyes opened, but otherwise he did not move until Frank said, 'You ready?' Then the outlaw turned his head and pulled his right hand from beneath his bedroll blankets. He was holding a sixgun in his fist. Before Frank and Charley recovered from surprise Smith cocked the weapon in their direction.

'I figured you'd try somethin' like this sooner or later,' Smith told Frank, ignoring the Indian. 'I'm goin' to blow you out of your boots if you come an inch closer.'

Frank gazed at the unshaven, vicious face beyond the gun; he knew without even trying it that offering an explanation would be like spitting into the ocean. John Smith would not even listen, let alone believe horsemen were approaching the Navajo camp looking for him. Trying to warn John Smith would be a waste of time.

Charley looked at Frank as though expecting Frank to have some words at his fingertips which would make John Smith lower the sixgun.

Frank had no such words, and as he stood broodingly regarding the other outlaw he tried to imagine how John Smith had got his hands on that sixgun.

Finally, feeling impelled to at least make an effort, he started to explain the predicament he and John Smith were in.

Smith snarled a violent interruption and swung the cocked Colt to also include the Navajo. 'You fellers are goin' to saddle me a horse and lead it to the bottom of this ledge, and you're not goin' to tell no one else what you're doing, because if you do, an' if them In'ians set up an ambush against me, I'm going to shoot some of those squaws and kids below the ledge where they're working. You understand?'

Charley looked at Frank again. Frank dolefully nodded his head at the man on the pallet. 'All right. Just let me say one thing: I wasn't tryin' to get your saddlebag. It's the gospel truth—there are riders coming.'

Smith waved the cocked Colt. 'I don't give a damn if the whole U.S. army is coming, you fetch that horse up to the ladder and don't tell a single soul what you two are up to. *Move!*'

CHAPTER SIX

WATCHERS

Frank did not open his mouth until he and the Navajo were on the ground at the base of the ladder, then he glanced upwards in the direction of the doorless little dark room and said, 'Two posses convergin' and now this. Charley, I got a feeling we're not goin' to come out of this too well off.'

The Navajo was troubled but silent as he led the way to the horses. Over there they encountered the woman who owned four of the horses and sixty sheep. She regarded Charley the longest and spoke to him with rising inflections. He answered shortly, and the woman looked at Frank and spoke in English.

'He wanted to see if he could walk.'

Frank nodded dully. He should have expected something like this. Yesterday Smith had asked about his weapons. Today he had found one of them.

The hefty woman said, 'I will get the gun from him.'

Frank frowned at her. 'Never mind.'

She returned Frank's gaze briefly, then set her back to him and studied the loose stock. She watched Frank and Charley go among the horses to catch one, and when they walked back she spoke in Navajo again, spoke to some length in what appeared to be a voice of urging. When Charley grunted an answer the woman spoke more fiercely this time and kept on until Charley rolled his eyes and glanced at Frank.

'She's got a bucking horse. What you call a spoiled horse. Anyone can ride him but no farther than he wants to go away from other horses. Then he bucks very hard.'

Frank eyed the woman, eyed Charley, and speculated. 'All that jabber meant she wanted Smith to ride her spoilt horse?'

'Yes. I told her it might not work, and if not the other outlaw would shoot someone. She said it would work because she would tie her other three horses over near the edge of the rancheria so he would not buck until he was out a ways.'

Frank eyed the woman again. She probably weighed two hundred pounds, although she was no more than average height for a female and like many fat people she had a clear complexion with almost no lines even though she had to be at least forty. In fact she was rather pretty.

She smiled at him. Frank fell to examining the horse they had brought back as he spoke to the woman. 'All right. Which is your mean horse?'

Charley knew the animal and turned stoically to go back for the spoiled horse. When they had a rope on the animal Frank stepped back to examine it. The horse was a stocking-legged dark sorrel no more than fourteen hands high but with heavy muscling. He weighed about fourteen hundred pounds. He was a good-looking beast; even his large brown eyes were gentle and intelligent-looking. Frank had encountered these animals before; once, they had been good using horses then someone had spoiled them. A horse built like the sorrel could buck, he had a short back with no spring in it, and powerful legs.

They led him back where the woman was waiting. She smiled, and spoke in English. 'I will trade him to you for your mule-nosed horse.'

Frank looked at the woman with hard eyes. 'I don't need a spoilt horse,' he said, urged Charley to start walking, and when they were midway toward the ladder he said, 'I got a feelin' about half your people can speak English.'

Charley had bleak humour in his glance, but said nothing.

At the ladder Frank said he would go up and fetch Smith's outfit and help saddle the sorrel horse. Charley was looking out through the trees where there was some kind of activity and nodded his head.

The moment Frank entered the little dingy room Smith recocked his sixgun, and Frank growled exasperatedly at him. 'Put that thing up before someone gets hurt. Can you walk?'

John Smith sneered. 'How do you think I found my gun? Sure I can walk.'

Frank watched the outlaw twist to have all his weight on his uninjured leg, then push upright still clutching the sixgun. Frank shook his head. Smith flared up at him. 'I didn't say I could dance a jig. You play tricks on me, cowboy, and you'll wish you hadn't.'

Frank raised his eyes to the other man's face.

'I'm not going to play any tricks on you. Nothin' would suit me better than to see you get clean away from here. Come along.'

'Wait a minute, cowboy. Shed the sixgun.'

Frank shook his head slowly. 'Naw, I don't think so. Now come along.'

'I'll blow your guts all over the wall. Shed that sixgun!'

Frank made no move to obey. In fact, he did not move at all, but he held the other man's glare when he spoke. 'Smith, I keep my gun. I told you there'd be no tricks. You're wasting time.'

Seconds ticked away as they faced each other. Frank had an eye on the finger inside Smith's trigger-guard; it did not tighten. He made a little crooked smile at the outlaw. 'Put up the gun and come along. You don't have that much time—and pick up your damned saddlebag.'

Frank turned his back and went as far as the door before pausing to look back. Smith had not moved, but now he did. He did not holster his handgun but he scooped up the fat saddlebag and limped toward the doorway.

He halted to gingerly poke his head out and peer around. Down among the trees people were going about their occupations as though they had no idea what was in progress on the ledge—which they hadn't. Out over the rancheria as far as a man could see the empty land shimmered in sun-brilliance.

Frank went as far as the ladder, then waited. Below, Charley was watching John Smith while holding tightly to the handsome sorrel horse. A few people turned to glance up, then looked away. They may have seen the gun hanging at John Smith's side, and the saddlebag clutched in his other hand but they acted as though none of this interested them, which was the Navajo way. After one glance John Smith no longer existed to them.

Frank offered a helping hand, but Smith snarled at him to go down the ladder first. Frank obeyed, halted at the bottom to watch the wounded man's face contort with pain as he descended one rung at a time, the descent made more awkward because both Smith's hands were full, and traded a glance with Charley.

Smith leaned on the ladder looking around. Sweat dappled his face, his breath was coming in short bursts. The wound was not causing him as much trouble as weakness was. He had been strong enough to prowl among the little rooms atop the ledge until he had located and retrieved his sixgun, but he was not strong enough for what he had just endured, climbing down a steep ladder to the ground.

When he met Frank's gaze he let go a rattling breath and straightened up. Frank said, 'You hadn't ought to try this, not for maybe another week anyway.'

Smith's unyielding glare lingered on Frank.

He did not open his mouth. He got ready to track on his good leg as he eyed the stocking-legged sorrel. Charley watched him from expressionless features, and off through the trees a fair distance the large woman who owned the stocking-legged horse was also watching him, but Smith probably did not notice her as he limped over to the horse.

No one offered to help Smith secure the saddlebag nor hitch his body around so he could toe into the stirrup.

He finally had to holster the sixgun in order to have both hands free, one for the mane the other for the horn. He looked around, gritted his teeth, toed into the stirrup and with a grim lunge rose upward to settle across leather. Frank could see his eyes darken with pain. He looked down and jerked his head for Charley to step away, then he evened up the reins and briefly looked around again. Only two nearby people were paying him the slightest attention. He said, 'Cowboy, if there's a bushwhack you're going to see some dead squaws an' pups.'

Frank walked forward. 'I told you—no tricks. I'll walk with you to the edge of the camp.'

There was a thin streak of blood on the back of Smith's leg visible through the slit trouser-leg. It was less blood than Frank would have expected under the circumstances.

They walked down through the grassy place

among the trees where no one even raised a head to watch. Frank saw Hosteen and the Roadman sitting together with a sack of tail hair between them pretending to be twisting up a hair rope. They did not look up either until Smith was past, then they put down the prickly strands and stoically watched.

A number of people watched from behind the sorrel horse including the hefty woman who owned the beast. When a pretty girl with light skin the colour of washed gold came soundlessly up beside her the hefty woman said in Spanish, 'A very bad man. Can you feel the badness?'

The girl's liquid black eyes watched the two white men and the horse as she replied. 'I can feel it.'

Frank saw two horses tied among the final fringe of trees and knew why they were there. He swung to glance in other directions out away from the trees; a brilliant, searing flash of distant light made him blink hard. Through slitted lids he looked again, but the flash was not repeated.

He knew what it was. So did every Indian who was among the trees blending with them. Frank raised an arm in the opposite direction, which was northeastward, and said, 'I can tell you this much: if you can make it, there's water and timber north of here.' He let his arm drop and raised his head toward Smith. 'That's the direction I rode from.'

Smith had his right palm resting on the butt of his beltgun as he squinted northward. Eventually he raked the land in other directions swiftly and looked down at Frank Walker. 'If you had a gawddamned brain in your skull you'd be ridin' with me.' His head jerked, the eyes suddenly blinking. 'What the hell was that?'

Frank shrugged. 'A sun devil. That's what these Indians call 'em.'

Smith sneered, spat and hauled the sorrel horse around, glanced over his shoulder, then dug in his heels. The surprised sorrel horse sprang ahead and came down running. By accident John Smith had done the one thing which would keep a spoiled horse untracked, he had busted him out and was forcing the horse to maintain his run. For the time being that was all the horse had on his mind, so he ran.

Two stalwart young Indians and Charley walked up beside Frank. Other Navajos drifted silently among the trees. The woman who owned sixty sheep and four horses brushed past and stopped close by on Frank's left side to watch. She was so surprised at the way her spoiled horse was obeying his rider that she breathed profanity in Spanish—she could not have cursed in Navajo because the language had no profanity in it.

Several of the statue-like people were looking in a different direction, and one of them, a grizzled, very dark, hawk-faced older man raised his arm. Sun devils were flashing southward, but now they were visible as horsemen; they had seen the fleeing man and were going in ragged, swift pursuit, fanning away from one another on an angling course of interception. They could have been two or three miles away, and they could have been farther, it was impossible to guess accurately in the glass-clear atmosphere.

Frank softly said, 'He wasted too much time, the damned fool.'

No one answered him. Moses Dominguez the Roadman came up through tree-shade with old Hosteen, feral eyes alight. In Spanish he said, 'No good, no good.'

The hefty woman muttered to herself something about Smith being unable to get away even if those strangers had not seen him, then she switched to English and said, 'A bad spirit but a strong one. By now he is bleeding hard.' She flashed a dark glance at Frank. 'I would sell that horse for eleven dollars.'

Frank did not answer, in fact he had scarcely heard her words. Around him Indians were peering intently ahead. The entire band was crowding among the trees to watch.

The spoiled horse was fresh, the mounts of Smith's pursuers were not. The damned fool had his sixgun; his Winchester had been left behind, but Frank did not think that mattered now. But his pursuers had Winchesters and the freshest horse on earth could not outrun a long-ranging carbine bullet.

Frank loosened a little at what he felt was a foregone conclusion. Behind him in the crowd someone made a little trilling sound. It did not mean anything to Frank, but the way the Indians standing around him reacted it meant something to them. He saw them twist quickly, every man and woman. He turned too.

Four armed men were back there with cocked carbines. They were in plain sight among the trees, close enough to oak trunks to have immediate shelter.

Movement to the left and right made heads turn slightly. Two more men, these kneeling beside trees with Winchesters snugged back to fire, were also aiming into the crowd of Navajos.

Silence as thick as night hung above the people. A few Indians were armed, but not many. Frank was armed and he was very good with weapons, but not even an idiot would move his right arm under these circumstances.

How those men had got in here without being seen or at least heard was understandable; everyone in the camp had been intent upon watching the fleeing man.

They had evidently split off from the main body of strangers and skulked in from the south where there were heavy shadows and many trees. It had been a successful stalk—for white men. It did not matter how they had known about outlaws being at the rancheria, but they had known otherwise they would not be waiting now for an excuse to start a massacre.

Frank studied as much of each white man as he could make out in the shdows, decided a thickly-made greying man with his hat tipped back and carrying an ivory-stocked Colt in his hip-holster might be someone in authority. He addressed this individual without raising his voice.

'All right, gents. You got the drop. No one's goin' to challenge you. What do you want?'

The grey man's eyes went to Frank's face and remained there for a long time before he answered. 'Who busted out of here on that sorrel horse?'

Frank's answer was not going to be satisfactory and he knew it. 'I don't know what his name was. I been callin' him John Smith.'

From a great distance came the faint but distinct little popping sounds of gunfire. It was more than one or two weapons, and for a brief time the little sounds ran together, then halted completely leaving no echoes in their wake.

CHAPTER SEVEN

CAUGHT!

The tense gunmen were willing for the greying man to be spokesman; they were too intent on watching for movement over their gunbarrels to spare even one word. They were heavily outnumbered even though only three or four of the people they were facing had guns showing. Also, they had their backs to the greater width and depth of the shady meadow and that was not a happy situation either. But they were clearly willing to start firing.

The greying man said, 'Who are you? What are you doin' here? There's a law against white men livin' among the In'ians. This is a reservation.'

Frank's answer was quietly offered. He did not feel that easy with all those guns pointing in his direction though. 'I was passing through. These folks had found a man on foot out yonder and brought him here to look after him.'

The greying man sarcastically said, 'Is that so? How was that feller hurt?'

'Shot through the upper leg. The Indians figured I might be able to help him. But the best I could do was wash the wound and bandage it. I'm not even very good at doctoring horses.'

While speaking Frank had been looking for a badge. He had found none. The greying man seemed to be loosening slightly, but his gunbarrel did not waver. 'What's your name?' he growled.

Frank had anticipated this question, had considered a number of names, and right at this moment did not believe the greying man had any idea who he was, which probably meant the other men, the ones who had been tracking him, were either still over on their barranca or were among the party which had gone flinging after John Smith. Instead of answering the question Frank asked one of his own.

'I was just goin' to ask you the same question, mister.'

The answer which came back was curt. 'Hank Duryea. That man who run for it—did he take anythin' with him?'

'Yes. A single saddlebag.'

'Do you know what was in it?'

Frank nodded. 'Money. It was full of the stuff.'

Finally, Hank Duryea lowered his Winchester. His companions took their cue from this and also lowered their gunbarrels. One of the kneeling men arose, looking at the greying man. 'Someone better go out there,' he said. Evidently this thought had also been in Duryea's mind because he said, 'Yeah. You go.

And Fred—bring back the saddlebag.'

Duryea leaned on his carbine gazing among the Indians. Evidently for the time being he was not going to press the issue of Frank Walker's name. He singled out old Hosteen and said, 'It's against the law to have white men here and you know it.'

Hosteen folded both arms across his chest and looked steadily back at Hank Duryea without making a sound. Duryea spat and faced Frank again. 'Which ones speak English?' he growled, evidently not unfamiliar with Navajo Indians. Frank nodded in Charley's direction. Duryea glared. 'Who's headman here?'

Charley looked toward his grandfather who was still standing defiantly in front of Duryea. The greying man then said, 'He knows the law, don't he?'

Charley shrugged.

Duryea frowned and spat aside for the second time, then faced Frank again. 'I'm from Bent's Crossing. That's a settlement about a hunnert miles south of here. An outlaw named Walt Younger shot three people during a bank robbery a couple of weeks back. Some fellers from town chased him up here then lost him.'

Frank acknowledged all that with a little nod of his head. 'Are you the constable or sheriff from down there?'

Duryea answered shortly. 'No. The son of a bitch killed our town marshal. The other two casualities was the bank president and a clerk.'

'How did you figure he'd be up here, Mister Duryea?'

'Some Messicans found a thoroughbred horse with a bloody saddle and brought him to town. A wounded man on foot in this kind of country can't go far. The closer I got up to this big mesa the more I figured where he might be hiding, and I was right.' Duryea glanced among the Indians again. 'They've had a rancheria in here since I was a little kid. I've never ridden into it before, but I've been past here a few times.'

Duryea looked behind himself, then at his slouching companions before he faced Frank again. 'How'd you come to be riding through here?'

Frank almost smiled. 'If I'd known what this country was like, believe me I'd have ridden in any other direction. I had an idea about finding some town down south where it didn't snow.'

One of the other men spoke for the first time. He had been studying Frank Walker. 'Hank, I'll lay you ten to one he's the feller those Coloradans are lookin' for.'

Duryea's answer indicated that this idea was not new to him. 'We'll wait until they get back here,' he told the other man, and gestured toward Frank. 'Drop the gun, mister.'

Frank was feeling fatalistic. He had known that sooner or later he would be disarmed, and now he also knew those four men who had been chasing him for the past three weeks were the ones who had gone after John Smith, probably because they had thought he would be Frank Walker. Until they arrived at the rancheria no one could prove who Frank was. He had maybe an hour to think of something clever. Right this minute he did not feel clever.

He dropped the gun.

Duryea looked stonily at Charley. 'Hiding a fugitive from the law can get you in all kinds of trouble.'

Charley almost made Frank smile. He showed unhappiness, even fear, in his face as he said, 'We live out here. No one can tell one white man from another, and that man was hurt so we brought him in to doctor him. He never told us he was an outlaw, mister.'

Duryea's lip curled; Frank could almost hear him thinking 'dumb damned In'ian'. He sent two men for the horse they had hidden south of the rancheria, then eyed Hosteen again. The old man was still standing like a stone image, arms crossed, black eyes fixed upon Duryea. Frank's urge to sardonically smile deepened. Old Hosteen too was acting the part of someone who neither understood what this was all about, or the language of the greying white man.

Duryea looked elsewhere and sighed. Then he abruptly said, 'What's your name, cowboy?'

Frank did not blink. 'Burt Chambers.'

Duryea gazed steadily at Frank. 'You're sure,

eh? It wouldn't be Frank Walker would it?'

'Who is Frank Walker?'

'Someone who shot it out with two rangemen up in a place called Fort Collins in Colorado, then ran for it.'

Frank cocked his head a little. 'Is that why someone wants him? Sounds to me like anyone who shoots it out with two men was just tryin' to stay alive, Mister Duryea.'

One of the other men strolled closer to Hank Duryea before grounding his carbine to lean on as he studied Frank. 'Seems like this Walker-feller was stealin' horses when those other two fellers come onto him. Self-defence under them circumstances don't count.'

Frank faced the speaker. 'And the law's after him?'

The rider continued to stare at Frank when he replied. 'The fellers who are after him are kinsmen of the two fellers he killed. There was six of 'em until Walker killed those two. They run a horse ranch up yonder. They want Walker. They don't want the law to get him.' The speaker suddenly grinned. 'And I think they're goin' to get him.'

The man's meaning was unmistakable.

The hefty Navajo woman who owned sixty sheep and four horses put a disgusted look upon the armed white men and spoke in English. 'You want somebody, you take 'em. Leave us alone. We don't want you here. This is our land. Today we will start a marriage ceremony. It is for Navajo only. You go.'

Hank Duryea and the men with him glared at the hefty woman. She abruptly started walking, brushed between Duryea and the grinning man and continued on her way. As though this were a signal the other Indians also began walking back up the grassy place toward the wide cleft in the shiprock-mesa. Even Charley walked away. Not one of the Indians looked at the armed white men they walked past.

The armed men looked back, then looked at Duryea; they were clearly not pleased at having Indians behind them, in fact they did not act as though they even liked being where they were. Duryea hoisted his carbine to the crook of an arm and growled at Frank. 'Come along. We'll go down near where we left our horses.'

Frank glanced downward. 'I don't like leavin' my gun lying here.'

Duryea signed for one of his companions to pick up the gun, then jerked his head for Frank to follow, and started walking.

Frank glanced over his shoulder. There was no sign of the men who had run John Smith to earth. By now there should have been—if they were coming to the rancheria. An idea suddenly occurred to Frank. He said, 'Mister Duryea, you got any idea how much money was in that saddlebag?'

The greying man put a hard look upon

Walker. 'Yeah, I got an idea. Why?'

'I was wondering. Those fellers who went after John Smith—or whatever his name was—do you know them very well?'

Duryea halted so abruptly a man back five feet almost rammed into him. He straightened up to his full height trying to see through the trees. Finally, without a word to anyone, Duryea went with thrusting strides out through the shadows eastward. One man hurried in his wake. Another man began to look slightly anxious, but he remained with Frank.

The men Duryea had sent for the horses walked up leading the animals and asked where Hank was going. Frank waited for the man near him to answer but nothing was offered from this rider until Duryea was lost out through the trees, then he said, 'I don't know. Them four Coloradans who went after Walt Younger ain't come back.'

One of the horsemen said, 'They will when they get finished out there. Why shouldn't they come back?'

Frank put the same question to the horse-holder he had put to Hank Duryea. 'You got any idea how much money was in that saddlebag?'

The reaction was identical, but a little slower arriving. The horse-holder turned a quizzical expression out through the trees, then he looked at Frank with a scowl. 'Naw. What the hell are you talkin' about? Them boys met up with us early this morning. They're manhunters the same as us.'

Frank smiled and nodded as though in agreement, then turned to face eastward as he said, 'You hear any horses; I sure don't.'

He got no answer.

Ten minutes later Hank Duryea and the man who had run after him strode back and without a word to the horse-holders grabbed their reins and pulled the horses around to be mounted. One of the horse-holders looked disbelieving when he said, 'Hey, Hank, what are you doing?'

Duryea answered with angry eyes. 'Get astride. Let's go see where those fellers are.'

The horse-holder jabbed with a thumb in Frank's direction. 'What about him?'

'The hell with him. Get on your horse. He's not our responsibility.'

They left Frank alone and sped among the trees riding eastward. Frank watched them go without smiling. He had not been simply trying to work a ruse; he was honestly of the opinion that those men who had overtaken John Smith no more than four or five miles eastward should have been in sight of the rancheria by this time. There was another reason why he had said what he did: he knew those four men, and clearly Duryea and his riding companions did not.

A quiet voice said, 'Where did they go?'

Frank turned and watched Charley approach. 'To look for the men who ran John Smith down.'

Charley was quizzical. 'They turned you loose?'

'They'll be back. Maybe they will. They didn't turn me loose they just happen to want that money more than they want me.'

Charley looked incredulous, but only for a moment, then he said, 'Come,' and when Frank took a last look out through the trees where horsemen were racing eastward in the direction of those earlier popping sounds, he repeated it with more urgency. 'Come!'

CHAPTER EIGHT

A TIME OF WAITING

The Indian had been right, no one would find him. The room where Charley left him was not on the ledge. It was not even part of the rancheria, it was along the northward face of the perpendicular stone wall of the shiprock beyond the trees and grass. Sunlight beat directly against the rising sweep of the mesa out there, but its most furious rays had no effect upon the little room carved of pure rock at the base of the mesa.

Directly in front of the room, which seemed more like a monk's cell than anything else, flourishing thornpin bushes grew horse-high and about five yards in width. Access to the room was by a narrow pathway behind the bushes.

When Charley had stopped and pointed to a cave-opening Frank thought to himself that no one would find this place in a dozen years of searching unless they knew where it was.

His quizzical look brought a response from the Navajo. 'Do you know the *anasazi*?'

Frank shook his head, leaning to peer into the cool, dark room.

'They were the old people. The very old people. They lived in all this country maybe a thousand years ago. No one knows where they came from or where they went.' Charley jutted his chin. 'They built the adobe rooms of our camp and they made this room through the stone of the cliff-face. It was a *kiva*, a sacred place only for men of the people.'

Frank pulled back and straightened up. 'Smells like a storehouse to me.'

Charley nodded. 'That's what the people have used it for since my grandfather was a child, but originally it was a *kiva*. Mostly, *kiva* were underground rooms with mounds of dirt for roofs above them. The *anasazi* made this one in solid rock.' Charley looked up the cliff. 'I don't know how they made it. They didn't have rock-drills or steel tools.' Charley returned his gaze to Frank. 'You stay in there until someone comes.' He abruptly walked back the way he had come following around the massive base of the shiprock.

Frank leaned to enter the stone room. Just beyond the door the roof was high enough for a tall man to stand erect. He had guessed why all door-openings were small; if there was an attack only one attacker could enter at a time and he would have to bend down to do it. The people inside could kill him and anyone who came after him, one at a time.

The room was surprisingly spacious considering that whoever had made it had had to hack his way through solid stone. Daylight was filtered through the thornpins which filtered out all direct light, and because the doorway faced eastward even if there had been no bushes daylight would reach the *kiva* for no more than perhaps three hours daily. The rest of the time its interior would be dark.

It was easily fifteen degrees cooler inside the stone hideout than it was outside, which would be a blessing at the peak of summer and a curse all the rest of the time.

Frank completed his exploration and returned to the sunlight behind the thornpin bushes. Behind him there had been nothing to sit on but the ground, so if *kivas* ever had furnishings they had disappeared long ago.

Otherwise, except for some almost indistinguishable art-work on the walls and smoke-stain on the ceiling, the stone room was empty and inhospitable.

He rolled a smoke from his diminishing supply of tobacco and papers, lit it and let sunlight warm him after he'd been chilled in the stone room.

A kangaroo rat no larger than a mouse darted around the stone doorway and disappeared inside the room. He paid no attention at all to the man, probably because he was not moving.

Occasionally sound would reach him from the rancheria. He could see all the eastward country for hundreds of miles, and there was no sign of Duryea or anyone else out there. If as Frank suspected those Coloradans who had been relentlessly tracking him for so long had opened that saddlebag, he would bet his mule-nosed bay horse, which was the most valuable thing he possessed, that they never even looked back. He knew those men, had known what they were before two of them had cornered him for a killing and had instead got killed themselves. But he could not have warned Duryea about them because if he had Duryea would have known he was not someone calling himself Burt Chambers, but was the man named Walker those Coloradans had been trying to hunt down, and Duryea's mood at their last confrontation was favourable toward the Coloradans and hostile to Frank. He would have handed him over without blinking an eye. They would have killed Frank on the spot.

He dropped the smoke, ground it out and continued to stand in filtered sunlight for a long while studying the enormous empty land. His guess was that a furious Hank Duryea was riding in pursuit of the men who now had the saddlebag full of greenbacks.

If he overtook them there would be one hell of a fight, but Frank wagged his head because he doubted that the men from that distant town would overtake the Coloradans, and if they came close Duryea might learn a lesson; those Coloradans would ambush him sure as hell. They were masters at things like bushwhacking.

Frank swung half around at the whispery sound of moccasins. The lady who owned sixty ewes and four horses—probably only three horses now—walked up and held out a water-jug. He accepted it and said, 'Thanks.'

She also had a food bundle which she put inside the low stone doorway, then she straightened around gazing steadily at him, and Frank sweated. She had the knack for making him distinctly uncomfortable even when she didn't open her mouth. He asked if the white men had returned. She flicked a black stare out across the empty land before answering in English.

'No. Four men went out to see.'

He frowned. 'From here?'

'Yes.'

Frank eyed the woman. Four more horsemen out there would be four more riders to attract attention. But he simply shrugged and also turned to look out where rising heat made a shimmery haze mile out.

'Big land,' she said, and he nodded without looking around. 'It was all water once.' He nodded again while continuing to look for movement. He did not know that it had all been covered with water once, and did not care. Like Frank, the hefty woman stood in filtered sunlight looking straight ahead. 'There is gold here,' she said and raised an arm in the direction of what appeared to be an area of uneven ground perhaps two or three miles northeastward. 'Do you see those mounds?' Frank saw them. 'Yeah.' She lowered her arm and held up her wrist which had no less than six or seven bracelets set with pale turquoise. 'Gold,' she said, singling out a particular bracelet which was especially massive and deeply engraved. 'You see?'

Frank leaned to look, eyes widening. He knew nothing about engraving or turquoise, but he knew gold, and this bracelet was at least three inches wide and quite thick. It looked ancient; some of the more shallow art-work had been worn nearly smooth. He straightened up, and the woman jutted her chin. 'From over there at those mounds,' she told him. 'Our people told of bearded dark men wearing steel hats and breastplates and riding mules who dug gold over there until their mules could carry no more, then they went away and never returned.' She looked at Frank. 'Spaniards. Maybe two hundred years ago. My grandmother found this bracelet over there.' She continued to stare at Frank. 'She told me where the gold lies over there, a streak of it in the rock as wide as a man's hand.'

Frank forgot about the Coloradans and Hank Duryea. 'Who's taken it out since those Spaniards left?'

'No one.'

He doubted her. 'What do you mean—no one? If your grandmother knew and you know—'

She was shaking her head before he finished speaking, black eyes fixed in the shimmery distance again. 'No Navajo. No white man because the people never tell their secrets to white men.' The woman raised speculative black eyes to Frank's face. 'Not you either.'

He studied her face for meaning, and she smiled at him, then removed the massive bracelet and offered it to him. He looked at the offering but made no move to accept it. Instinct told him that heavy circlet of ancient gold would not come to him without requirements, and he suspected what they might be so he shook his head and smiled at her. 'It is yours and you keep it. It belongs in your family.'

For a long moment their eyes held, then she slowly pulled the bracelet back into place on her arm, and when she raised her eyes again their expression was different—not angry, not hurt, but different. She let her gaze drift back out across the distance again and said, 'Nobody goes there. No one will take the gold. All things have spirits; the dead have very strong spirits, even rocks and buttes, even this high mesa has a spirit. Out there where the ground was ripped and torn there are many spirits to reseal the earth and heal it. If you went over there to dig, they would spoil your water, make your horse run away, hide your food. They would make you die.' She looked up again. 'You don't believe that. Ask Hosteen. People have found the place. Ask Hosteen what became of them. No one goes near there now. But if you want gold from over there you can have the bracelet.'

He considered her smooth face and even, soft features. Once, she had been a beautiful woman. He smiled at her. 'No, I won't go out there and I won't tell anyone about the place. What is your name?'

She murmured in her native language, saw Frank's blank look and said, 'If you stayed you would learn. My name is Annabelle. That was as close as they could come to it at the school.' Then, without warning, she also said, 'I will go now,' and walked away.

It was probably just as well because Frank was beginning to sense a strange feeling about her in himself. He turned back to watching the land. It was as monotonously empty as it usually was.

He made a slow look in all directions, then tipped down his hat and said aloud, 'Now I can make it. Go south and ride all night an' when they find my tracks that's all they'll find.'

He was turning to duck through the stone doorway, but paused for another long look far out in the direction of those distant low mounds; in Colorado and Wyoming miners called them 'tailings'. Only the Lord knew what Indians called flung-up dirt from excavations. If what that woman had said was true, and he thought it could be true, then when he saddled up and headed south he would probably never again be as close to being a rich man as he was today.

He ducked through the doorway with his water and food, and two kangaroo rats ran frantically toward the opening; evidently they lived in this room, or at least had until Frank had scairt the daylights out of them.

The water was tepid, but it was wet. The food was some kind of crumbly cornbread and goat meat. He had never been a finicky eater, and since it had been a long time since his last meal he sat down in the gloom to fill up on what

Annabelle had brought.

His decision to run for it had not come suddenly. It had occurred to him at the south end of the rancheria when those men from Bent's Crossing had gone racing away leaving him standing there. But he had wanted enough time to lapse with no sign of their return to make him confident that he had a good chance of not being caught again.

That much time had elapsed; that was why he had stood outside for so long watching for riders. Now, having eaten and with shadows on their way, he was ready. His only cause for worry was his barefoot horse, but that could not be helped nor corrected; it was an easy matter to pull shoes, almost any tool would do for that, but putting shoes back on a horse required particular kinds of tools, and new nails.

He arose and placed the water-jar and earthen plate outside the door of his hiding-place, stepped ahead to make a final scan of the empty land, saw nothing that resembled riders, caught no sign of movement, and turned to walk along the base of the cliff in the direction of the horse-area. He was confident and he was also alive to danger if he was making a miscalculation, but mostly he was eager to make the effort.

Indians might be satisfied to spend their lives in isolated places like this generation after generation but most white men were not.

He saw slow movement ahead among the trees and out through the grassy place where the people worked, and he heard sheep bleating over the more strident noises made by goats where a band was being driven toward the fenced-in places for the night. The smell of sheep was strong in this place even when there were no sheep around.

He looked ahead, to his left and right, and once or twice back the way he had come, but he never once looked up.

There was pale smoke rising from a square hole in the top of a large room on the ledge. He thought it would be from a cooking fire and did not envy anyone standing over a fire as hot as this day had been. He had forgotten entirely about the Roadman and the Navajo wedding.

There were very few people around. In fact, the area where the horses grazed did not even seem to have the children guarding it as was usually the case. He wondered mildly at the absence of Navajos, but since he did not want to face any of them as he was saddling his bay horse, not even Charley for whom he had developed a liking, he felt more relief than curiosity.

The bay horse was sleek. Even though the grass was shorter than the grasses Frank was accustomed to, it evidently had great strength to it. His horse looked better now than he had looked in more than a month.

The bay stood stoically to be rigged out, his attitude clearly one of resignation; he had come to like this hidden place very much.

Frank led him around through the trees toward the south, being mindful of avoiding all the open places even though he was aware that if anyone wanted to see him they could. Two fat puppies who had been falling over each other in simulated battle, growling fiercely and rolling up lips to show milk-teeth, broke off to sit up and search for the source of the man-smell. When they finally saw Frank they watched his progress with intent interest and forgot to bark.

He got down where the riders from Bent's Crossing had abandoned him, and paused to look back. He knew he should have thanked the people, especially Hosteen and Charley, and the hefty woman who owned sixty ewes and four horses. He hoped they would not feel badly that he had chosen to depart without expressing gratitude, but he also knew that if he sought them to explain that he was leaving they would try to talk him out of it and that would have been even more awkward, so he swung into the saddle, turned his back on the secret oasis and rode down to the last trees beyond which lay raw and naked country.

Just before leaving the shade he halted, twisted to look back, and raised his right arm in a high salute he thought no one saw, then settled forward and rode out into the sunlight.

He had not been at the rancheria very long, but evidently he had unconsciously become accustomed to its shade and seclusion; half a mile out he began to feel almost naked. He was visible for miles if anyone happened to be looking.

A full mile out he thought he heard a faint whistling sound, glanced all around, then shrugged and continued on his way, but the sentinel atop the mesa who had whirled the bird-bone to make that sound and who had been watching everything Frank had done since he'd left the *kiva* was not signalling Frank's departure. When Hosteen emerged bare from the waist up and covered with glistening sweat from the ceremonial room on the ledge and walked out to the edge before glancing up, the sentinel high above him stopped making his whistling sound and pointed a rigid arm northward, then he made the hand-arm sign for 'riders coming'.

CHAPTER NINE

A SHOCK!

If Frank had waited another fifteen minutes he would have seen the riders; as it was when he left the trees his vision back beyond them was cut off and the farther he went the more that huge hulking shiprock blocked out his rearward view. He rode steadily but slowly, satisfied that he would be safe from pursuit at least until sundown. After that he would be even safer, and with a little luck—and no tender hooves under him—he might see the rooftops of that town Duryea hailed from come daylight.

He was a tiny moving speck, a flea crossing a huge tan belly. The bay horse walked along at his own gait, agreeable to the exercise he was getting and indifferent to almost everything because there was nothing worth looking at unless there was movement, which might mean snakes, and there was none.

Frank looped both reins and considered his slack tobacco sack. He still had six or seven brown wheatstraw cigarette papers but there was only enough tobacco left for two smokes—three if he made them less full-bodied than was his custom.

He and the horse had food and water in them, and as the day headed along toward its slow ending the heat would diminish; neither the man nor the animal should be suffering very much by the time they saw rooftops.

At least that was Frank Walker's opinion.

He dozed from time to time, looked far out occasionally, and even once twisted to look back. The land was exactly as it had been since before time could be counted, empty, endless, utterly silent and ageless. He wagged his head; perhaps if a man had been born here and had never been anywhere else he would be satisfied. Otherwise he would dearly miss the sound of running water, big fragrant trees, and prairies of grass.

He had never been down over the line into Mexico, and although that had been his first thought after the killings he had had reservations from the beginning. Subconsciously he liked the idea of being close enough to the border to be able to duck over it if he had to, while at the same time feeling a reluctance to do so otherwise.

Somewhere down south there was livestock country. He'd known a number of riders in the north country who had ridden for outfits on the South Desert.

His horse abruptly missed a step, which jarred the slouching man on his back. A small red-grey fox no larger than a good-sized house-cat appeared over the lip of a shallow gully, turned to stone for a moment of absolute astonishment, then exploded into a wildly frantic run, his brush acting as a rudder as he zig-zagged around rocks and uneven places. Frank laughed; there was no echo. The horse followed the flight of the small animal with a sour expression; it had startled him out of a half-doze.

Frank told the bay horse that there was

native life in this barren world after all. The horse did not even cock his ears backwards at the sound of a human voice. He was still disgruntled.

A lowering sun mantled distant and widely scattered upthrusts of sandstone which seemed to arise directly from the ground for no particular reason with a softly purple colour which had a blending of pink in it. That much, Frank admitted to himself as he studied the scattered plinths in fading daylight, was beautiful—if a man wanted to sit around every day waiting for desert sunset.

It was not until he decided to keep his horse from dozing by loping for a mile or so that something told him to look back. There was four of them far beyond rifle-range but clearly dogging his tracks. Undoubtedly they had seen him hours ago. Hair stiffened on the back of his neck. Duryea'd had more than four riders with him; he'd had at least seven and maybe more. Frank had never seen them all.

Four men on his trail meant the same Coloradans who had persistently, doggedly and grimly been trying to catch and kill him for almost a month.

The surprise and shock passed swiftly. He had no idea how they happened to be back there, but it did not require very much speculation to arrive at a probable conclusion. They had somehow or other eluded the men from Bent's Crossing, had resumed their manhunt, probably with John Smith's saddlebag full of money divided among them by now. Frank shook his head. That kind of perserverance was rare, very rare, but those men were nothing if they were not rawhide and deadly vindictive.

He held to the lope and studied the onward country. If he could remain far ahead until nightfall he could elude them. It was encouraging that they did not also lope. Their horses had to be worn down by now. If a man killed his saddlehorse in this country from overriding he might damned well be committing suicide.

He began to feel better once he'd made his observations, but it still bothered him that they were back there. Hell, they must have returned to the rancheria and picked up his sign no more than a half-hour after he'd started south. And he'd been so damned clever, giving them and Duryea's crew plenty of time to get a long way northward.

He slackened off to a steady walk. His pursuers were so distant they looked like ants. If they managed to reach that town down yonder they would get fresh animals; one thing was damned certain, they were never going to stop until they caught him.

He told the bay horse they might not even be safe crossing the line down into Mexico. The bay horse did not even know there was anyone behind them. He was approaching a long swale which was about a quarter mile wide. It was not deep, just deep enough to hide a rider and his horse. Some other time it might have provided a sheltering place, but not now. Those four Coloradans would never be deluded by a man they could not see; as long as they had good horse-tracks to follow they would ride right up to the gates of Hell and shoot off the hinges if Frank Walker was behind the gates.

That distinctive pink-purple glow turned slightly darker as time passed. When Frank rode up out of the wide arroyo still heading southeasterly, the nearest massive finger of rigid stone was greying, losing its beauty, becoming uniquely grey and aloof. He could have passed within ten yards of it simply bearing to the left a few degrees; instead he passed it from farther out.

They continued to appear, spaced widely, with almost as many different shapes and heights as there were plinths. He had a feeling of riding across something like Purgatory. The farther a man rode the more the sameness of the country continued to lie ahead and on all sides of him. There were patches of scrub brush and grass, usually on the sheltered sides of the sandstone spires, but not enough to support very many animals.

He sat sideways looking back. The

manhunters had gained a little but nowhere nearly enough to use weapons. Even if they'd had long-ranging rifles instead of saddle-carbines, they could not have come close to reaching Frank.

Dusk arrived very slowly, grudgingly, and it lingered longer than Frank would have thought it might. In the north country nightfall dipped down on the shirt-tails of the dusk. Out here although dusk gradually shaded toward darkness it was one hell of a long, drawn-out process.

He would reach that town well ahead of the manhunters; might even have an hour or two to buy food and strike out again, and, much as he hated the idea, he would have to leave his horse behind because it would require too much time to wait for a shoeing job.

He did not have a lot of money, but he had enough. It was not the idea of spending money on a fresh horse that troubled him, it was the idea of abandoning an old friend.

The farther he rode as the endlessly lingering dusk hung on, the more slow anger built up within him. He had never been a quick-tempered man. Things built up in Frank Walker for a long time. To other men it had seemed an inordinate length of time. A few had seen him angry, but very few. He was an even-tempered, shrewd, reasonable man who understood more than people suspected. He was also a dead shot with a handgun or a Winchester. Right now, glancing back unable to see far enough through dusk to sight his pursuers, his anger was becoming something solid and constant.

So far those manhunters had made him ride hard, hide often, live poorly, and keep watch over his shoulder. Before they were finished they were going to make his existence even more miserable.

He squared round in the saddle, watched the shadows, studied the nearest sandstone upthrusts, stood in his stirrups for a sighting of rooftops even though he knew he had not covered enough ground yet to see them at dusk, then eased back down in the saddle and rolled a smoke, his expression harsh.

He briefly thought of Duryea and his town-riders, spat in scorn, and concentrated on himself and the men back yonder. That was all that mattered in this timeless empty silence he was riding through. If they caught him out here they would not even have to bury his carcass; it could lie until it turned to a grinning skull discernible through skin like dehydrated parchment, and the chance of anyone, even a Navajo, coming past to find his body was as remote as the stars.

He looked upwards. There were a few pale stars, darkness was still not entirely down. More stars would appear in an hour or two. He lowered his head, scowled and raised it again, eyes intent this time.

There was a high veil up there, through it stars looked wet, their light being diffused by the thin overcast. 'Rain,' he said aloud. 'By gawd I don't believe it, not in this country.'

But the linen-like overcast covered all the sky he could see, and it was the kind of a moist mistiness that in any other place he had been signified oncoming rain.

A fresh series of idea filled his mind. If it rained it would wash out his tracks, the only things those killers yonder could use to find him.

He tipped up his face again trying to taste or scent water in the thickening night. If there was a scent he could not discern it, but sure as hell that mistiness was increasing because even though he could not see it now he could see the stars shining through it, and they were like milk.

His pursurers would be aware of the situation if rain fell. He knew them well enough to know they were shrewd, resourceful men.

Riding in this strange void of a lightness night was like riding in limbo. He could not even make out the shiprocks and other plinths until they loomed like enormous giants dead ahead.

His horse was not favouring—yet—and in fact he acted about as strong as he had when they had first ridden away from the rancheria. Frank's confidence rose a notch. He became increasingly confident that by dawn the manhunters would have no idea where he had gone, and if it did not rain they would have to turn back to find where he had branched off.

But his confidence was diluted by anxiety over where he was, where he was going, and when if ever he and his horse would find water, because he was hopelessly lost.

CHAPTER TEN

BLUE HOUSE

When the rain came it was more noticeable for the hissing sound it made against the crusted and moistureless earth than for its wetness. For a while anyway, then it increased to a constant warm-water deluge and remained that way.

Frank shrugged into his old jacket from behind the cantle, buttoned it to the gullet and set his hat squarely, something he did instinctively because he was accustomed to wind with rainfall, but in this country there was no wind, just rain which came straight down.

He rode humped up; darkness was everywhere. He could have ridden right up to a high cliff and off it, if there had been cliffs.

He thought of the men pursuing him. If the rainfall continued throughout the night and they reached that town back yonder and failed to find him there, they would be furious.

Their choices would be simple; lose Frank Walker's tracks when the rain washed them out, and thus lose the man they had been trying to get close enough to shoot to death for a month, or, try to overtake him in the darkness on horses unable to absorb much more abuse without collapsing. He was certain they knew there was a town ahead; if Duryea's men had not told them the Indians might have. If they rode their horses to death in overtaking Frank—and did not find him in the darkness—they would have lost all they had been straining to achieve for a month. He would get away and they would probably never find him again. If they rode their horses to death and *did* catch Frank, the walk to that town would be worth while. They could buy new animals and turn back toward Colorado leaving behind a riddled body no one would find for many years.

He let their choices go and boosted the bay horse over into a slow lope that covered miles without tiring the animal.

And in the heavy darkness without stars or a moon showing through that high veil, he changed course, heading southwesterly now instead of southeasterly toward Bent's Crossing.

He too was taking a large gamble. The crusty abrasiveness of this land would wear hooves down quickly, particularly if they were hooves accustomed to wearing shoes and had become soft as a result of that.

Nor did he have any idea where he was going nor what he might find when dawn returned. What he *did* know was that his pursuers would not be able to read tracks until dawn, and meanwhile since he had been heading straight for that town none of them had ever seen, they would probably continue in that direction. If the rain did not slacken off, when they turned back his passage would have been obliterated.

Water seeped under the old coat, which was not waterproof but which had been adequate to turn light rain; but this was not a light downpour. It never achieved the status of a deluge, it simply continued to come down hour after hour. Long after his tracks had been washed away, it was still coming down. In fact, by the time a soggy dawn arrived, grey and dismal, it was still coming down. By then Frank was fairly well soaked beneath the coat.

Visibility increased with grudging slowness. At first all he could discern was exactly what he had been looking at since riding down off the westerly barranca into this eerie wasteland, and even when there was something to look at he did not see it until his horse raised its head, ears pointing directly ahead.

Frank strained, hoping it would be a village. Instead it was a large drive of Navajo sheep, goats, and horses with the people out on both sides and in the drag. He reined to a halt, made no attempt to estimate the number of driven animals beyond noticing there was one hell of a lot of them scattered over about a half mile, and guessed from the number of mounted Indians that what he had come upon was an entire Navajo band on the move.

There were a lot of Indians. They had seen him before he had seen them, and while watching him as they straggled past, made no move to ride out to meet him, nor even to raise an arm here and there in the customary range-country salute.

He did not present a good appearance, wet, unshaven, grey in the face with lines around the eyes from lack of rest. The Indians preferred to ignore his distant presence as though he did not exist, an attitude he was learning to accept as a Navajo characteristic, but if he allowed these people to pass without meeting at least one of them he might meet no other people. He was concerned with where he was, so he raised his right arm and urged the bay horse over into a slow walk heading for the middle of the drive where four Indians with carbines were riding. They halted the moment Frank started toward them; they evidently had been watching him and discussing his presence.

He halted a hundred or so yards away, lowered his arm, nodded gravely and spoke in English. 'Good morning. I am lost. I came from the north and during the storm last night—' He smiled and gestured.

The four Indians were young men, dark, expressionless. They wore their hair in the traditional Navajo way. There was no sign in their attire that they had been influenced by white customs. He began to think they had not understood his words. But one man leaned forward with both hands on the fork of his saddle and said, 'You are about seven miles from Blue House settlement.' He jutted his chin. 'That way.' The Indian's black eyes were full of frank curiosity. 'Where, north, did you come from?'

With no intention of telling his story Frank made a vague gesture as he answered. 'Back where there are some low hills north and west.'

The Indians showed nothing, so it was impossible for Frank to determine whether they believed him or not, but the man leaning on his saddle said, 'This is a reservation. White men are not supposed to be here. There is an Indian constable at Blue House. You had better say you came from the west and got lost in the night.'

That ended it. The four bucks rode ahead to resume their place in the drive, leaving Frank looking after them. He would have liked to know how much distance there was between the Blue House settlement and the town of Bent's Crossing.

He shrugged and started ahead. Seven miles was a very short distance in relation to the number of miles he had already ridden.

Even so the sun was burning through frayed rain-clouds before he saw the place. By the time he rode in from the west, steam was rising and sun-heat contributed to mugginess.

Blue House settlement was a Navajo community. People turned to watch the solitary white man on his bay horse go down the single broad roadway. The village was not really very large, but its structures were scattered without much order so it appeared larger.

He did not expect to find a saloon nor a rooming-house but he hoped there might be a blacksmith shop. There was none, but there was a thick-walled, massive adobe trading-post operated by a paunchy, shrewd-eyed white man who emerged from his store in response to a whispered warning to watch Frank ride through town. When Frank was abreast the thick man called to him.

'Hey, cowboy, you lost?'

Frank turned toward the tie-rack. 'You got it right,' he answered, reining up and swinging to the muddy roadway, wearing a wide grin. 'Damnedest country I ever stumbled into; it all looks the same even in broad daylight. In the dark—' He looped his reins and leaned on the rack appraising the heavy-set older man. 'The name is Chambers, Burt Chambers.'

The trader's tawny-tan eyes examined Frank slowly and minutely before he said, 'Glad to meet you, Mister Chambers. My name is Art Wheeler. We don't see many whiteskins out here. Come inside and I'll set you up to a sarsparilla. It's against the law to sell anything stronger on an In'ian reservation.'

Frank did not move. 'Is there a place a man might look after his horse, Mister Wheeler?'

The older men nodded and jerked a thumb. 'Round back of the store I got some corrals. Feed's dear in this country; it'll cost you two bits.'

Frank handed over the silver coin and led his horse around back under the speculative gaze of Arthur Wheeler, who turned to pad back into his store as a young Indian wearing sleeve-protectors made of thick brown paper came up to murmur into Wheeler's ear. The trader nodded his head.

Behind the trading-post there was a network of faggot corrals; it seemed that Mister Wheeler also traded in livestock. Frank cared for his horse, stood briefly watching him greedily eat then headed for the rear entrance of the trading-post. He had the feeling of being watched. That too seemed to go with being in Navajo country.

Inside, the trading-post smelled faintly of some kind of spice, perhaps cloves. There was one window in the front wall and no windows anywhere else, which made the place shadowy, and it was full of Navajo rugs, saddle-blankets, even ponchos and Indian silver, the latter mostly hanging from back-wall and ceiling-pegs.

Art Wheeler was smoking a Mexican cigar and leaning on a counter near his cash drawer, evidently waiting, when Frank walked in shrugging out of his soggy jacket, which weighed three times as much wet as it weighed dry. Wheeler shifted position and set up a bottle of molasses-coloured sarsparilla. He did not bring forth a bottle for himself. His features were friendly without the shrewd eyes managing to achieve the warmth of his smile as he said, 'If you're low on supplies I got 'em.'

Frank tasted the drink, thanked Wheeler for it and asked for a couple of sacks of tobacco and some papers. As the trader turned away to get those items he spoke casually over his shoulder. 'Darned seldom whites come through here; I been here for eleven years an' you're only the second one I ever had ride in on us from the north.'

Frank considered the trader's broad back. He had ridden in from the west; he had purposefully not ridden in from the north.

As Wheeler returned with the little sacks and

papers Frank counted out coins for them, then reached for his soft drink. Wheeler picked up the coins as he said, 'That other feller was maybe four, five years back an' he was in a hurry to get down to the Mex border.' Wheeler raised sly eyes and grinned.

Frank said, 'How far is it?'

'Three days' ride,' the trader replied, his smile fading slightly to be in part replaced by the look of a man who had just received confirmation to a suspicion.

Frank looked straight at Wheeler. 'I'm not running from the law.'

Wheeler accepted that with a slight shrug of fleshy shoulders. 'Mister Chambers, look around; this store keeps me so busy I don't have time to mind other folks' business.'

Frank rolled a smoke. 'Is there a blacksmith around?'

Wheeler pursed his lips. 'These people almost never shoe their horses. Mostly, their critters got feet like iron. I got a man who works for me now and then who can shoe. I'll send for him. He can meet you out back. He'll charge you a dollar—I know that's high, Mister Chambers, but you know how them things work. There's only this one shoer and your horse needs a set.' Wheeler grinned. 'If you figure to lie over and rest up for a day or two, I got a cabin that I rent out by the night—four bits in advance.'

Frank met the trader's gaze, and laughed. Wheeler understood and joined in. He evidently was an individual who could see humour in his own avariciousness. He said, 'Mister Chambers, there ain't many things that'd keep a white man in a place like this; makin' a little money is one of them.'

Frank shoved the empty bottle away. 'You got all the bets covered,' he said, still amused, and the older man nodded his head and straightened up off the counter to call the young Indian who seemed to serve as a clerk. He told him in Spanish to fetch the horse-shoer.

Frank bought some food and took it out back to eat near the corral. A few Indians saw him and no doubt wondered, but their nature was to show no curiosity, nor even for that matter to gaze at a stranger for more than a fleeting moment.

The heat was increasing, his horse had rolled and was back eating again. The flies which hovered did not bother him, but some mud-daubers gathering wet soil over beside the leaky stone trough did. He sidled up for a drink as though each hornet was a ten-foot rattlesnake.

Frank draped the soggy jacket from a corral post and squatted in half-shade, half-sunlight, to have a meal. Hunger was something that had never bothered him until he began eating, then it seemed to arrive all at once.

He heard the Indians coming before he looked up at them. One was the clerk from the post, the other was a rawboned, slightly stooped man with a heavily lined face and traditionally long hair worn clubbed in back and held in place by a headband. He eyed Frank with reddish-brown eyes of particular brightness. He was carrying some blank horseshoes, a short length of railroad-track which was the Navajo equivalent of an anvil, and a rolled-up shoeing apron of scarred horsehide inside of which were his tools.

He spoke no English so the store-clerk interpreted for him. The shoer wanted to know if Frank's horse kicked, bit, or struck. Frank shook his head and arose to take them into the corral, loop a rope and tie the horse to be shod. He went completely around lifting all four feet as he moved and striking them with his fist. The shoer nodded satisfaction and went up to talk to the horse, then step back and unroll his apron.

Frank and the clerk left the corral, the clerk heading for the store and Frank hunkering down to finish his meal.

In an hour he would be on his way. He thought.

The sky was beginning to pale-out a little so he studied it for the veil which not uncommonly followed, but this time it did not appear which left Frank to assume that the paleness meant rising heat. He finished eating, forgot about the weather, sat flat down with shoulders against the knobby faggots of dead wood which made the corral's wall, and relaxed.

He was less tired than sleepy. He dozed while considering some things that seemed to have lost their peril for him, which included the four Coloradans who were probably over in Bent's Crossing by now mad as wet hens. He also considered his future, and where he would ride when he left the Navajo settlement. The trader would be able to give him some idea of the country roundabout.

He tipped down his hat, belched, settled more comfortably against the corral and wondered about the future. He was a tophand; for his kind finding work was never very difficult. He could perhaps make a leisurely sweep southwesterly and wind up over in California, a place he had heard much about but had never felt any particular desire to see, until now.

The Indian tapped away with his shoeing hammer in the corral, making wood-pecker sounds, over on the far side of the settlement westward a dog fight erupted but lasted only a few moments, and someone driving an old wagon rattled his way up through from the south.

Frank fell asleep as the heat grew, and sweated without being aware of it. The humidity was high and the atmosphere was breathless.

Around in front the Navajo with his brown-paper sleeve protectors sauntered out of the store to kill a few minutes looking around. He faced northward and gradually stiffened as he stared, then turned abruptly and hurried back inside. The trader was scowling over a dog-eared old ledger when the youth came up and breathlessly said, 'Mister Wheeler—four white men are coming into town from the north.'

Wheeler raised round eyes. That made five white men in one day. He closed the book, put aside the pencil-stub and arose to pad out front to see for himself. By the time he got out there the four strangers were coming down the roadway. They were stained, faded, heavily armed men who needed shaves and shearings. He stepped back into the gloomy doorway where they would not see him at once, and met the dark stare of his clerk. Wheeler was beginning to have a very bad feeling.

It was not helped by the sudden absence of Indians out in the muddy roadway. One thing Art Wheeler had learned in his eleven years among them was that they possessed an uncanny sensitivity. They too had been unsettled by this sudden influx of hard-looking, beard-stubbled, shaggy-headed, heavily armed white men. There was not a Navajo in sight.

CHAPTER ELEVEN

THE ARRIVALS

All four of the weathered and stained horsemen tied up out front and sauntered into the trading-post. One seemed older than the others, at least he was grey and wrinkled around the eyes and his bearing was thoroughly self-confident, as though he had seen it all at least once.

As his companions fanned out through the store, looking, the greying man approached the counter near the cash drawer where Art Wheeler had a fixed smile in place. These men were dangerous; they were probably outlaws, and four such individuals posed a genuine threat. His bad feeling had been increasing since he'd got a close look at them. He said, ''Morning. My name's Art Wheeler.'

The rawboned greying man nodded over that and asked for four sacks of tobacco, and as Wheeler went to get them the greying man said, 'That was one hell of a storm last night, eh?'

Wheeler agreed as he turned back with the little sacks. 'For a fact. When it rains in this country it comes all at once, then there ain't no more for maybe six months. That'll be fifteen cents.'

The greying man counted out coins and put them down. His eyes glowed with insincere amiability. 'We been on the trail for a spell, Mister Wheeler,' he said, looking steadily at the man across the counter from him. 'Last night we lost a feller we been lookin' for until some In'ians drivin' a big bunch of sheep came along over west of Bent's Crossing. They met a horseman headin' in this direction about dawn this morning.' The greying man who had not given his name paused to settle low on the counter methodically rolling a cigarette, eyes on his work. He licked the paper, curled it, twisted the end and popped it between his lips, then flicked a sulphur match while gazing at Wheeler and said, 'We found some tracks out a ways. They come straight down here.' The greying man dropped his match and exhaled grey smoke. 'You havin' the store and all, and him most likely needin' vittals—' The greying man lowered his cigarette, smiling steadily at Art Wheeler. He was waiting.

Art sweated. If Mister Chambers walked in about now—If he lied to these men and they found Chambers—He said, 'They got lawmen over in Bent's Crossing. Maybe they'd know something about this man.'

The unshaven hard-eyed stranger was comfortable against the counter. 'Well sir, Mister Wheeler, we never went into the place. Y'see we run onto some fellers from there, a man named Duryea and some friends of his, and we didn't get along so well, so we was speculatin' over there and seen those In'ians makin' their drive and talked to 'em. Then we come over here.' The greying man dropped ash. 'Good thing we met 'em or we maybe never would have found this son of a bitch.'

Art Wheeler still had not made his decision so he tried to gain a little more time by saying, 'What'd he do?'

'Murdered two men up in Colorado.'

Wheeler's eyes widened. 'Really? Then you boys'll be lawmen?'

The greying man's smile returned. 'You could say that, Mister Wheeler. Now then, when was he here?'

The temptation to lie was very strong, but the problem with sending them on a wild-goose chase was that when they discovered he'd lied to them they would come back. Art Wheeler had lived on the frontier all his life. He knew the kind of men he had to deal with in the store this morning. Nor was it as difficult to arrive at his personal degree of involvement in all this after the rawboned, lined older man had mentioned murder.

He sighed and fished in a pocket for his plug of tobacco, bit off a corner, got it settled in his face, repocketed the plug and said, 'I didn't catch your name, friend.'

The greying man's false amiability was

slipping. 'I didn't tell you my name—but it's Uriah Kimball, an' Mister Wheeler, me'n my brothers aren't real patient men. When was Frank Walker here?'

Wheeler stared. 'Chambers. There was a man in town named Burt Chambers. I never heard of no one named Frank Walker.'

The greying man did not bat an eye. 'All right; when was Burt Chambers here?'

Wheeler heard the other strangers talking to his clerk over by the case which held guns and shot them a glance. His Navajo had gone impassive, a sure sign he was unsettled. One of the strangers was examining a new Colt sixshooter with the other two leaning comfortably watching.

Wheeler turned back and spoke in a lowered voice. 'He's still here, Mister Kimball.'

They greying man rocked back, dropped his smoke and stamped it onto the oiled floor. When he raised his head there was no surprise in his face, just satisfaction. 'Where?' he asked softly.

Wheeler had gone this far so he went farther and jerked a thumb. 'Out back gettin' his horse shod.'

'Is that a fact? What colour horse?'

'Mule-nosed bay. Rode down a little but a real quality animal.'

Uriah Kimball made a little bark of a laugh. 'Yes, he sure is a good horse; he's been stayin' ahead of us for a long time.' Kimball continued to lean on the counter, his mind obviously busy as he turned slightly to watch his companions. While doing this he quietly asked what kind of law there was in Blue House settlement.

'A big Navajo constable,' Wheeler replied.

Kimball turned his head slowly. 'That's all?'

Wheeler nodded. 'Yes. In these reservation settlements that's usually all they have. At the agency they got regular U.S. deputy marshals and Indian police, but in a place like this where there's hardly ever any trouble—'

Kimball nodded his head. 'How about these here In'ians, Mister Wheeler; are they peaceable folks—mind their own business and all, do they?'

Wheeler nodded. 'When you rode into town they went to their shacks. I guess you didn't notice that.'

Kimball had noticed. 'Yeah, we did. Now then, I want to tell you something, friend—stay here in the store. I don't give a gawddamn what you hear, stay inside.' Uriah Kimball drew up off the counter without a shred of his smile remaining. 'Out back is he? What's out there?'

'Some corrals. I buy an' sell sheep, goats, horses and whatnot on the side. He wanted his horse shod an' he bought some grub to eat while he was waiting. It's the biggest corral, the round one.'

Kimball nodded, looking steadily at Wheeler.

'Now then, you walk to the back door and look around out here. If he's still there, you maybe wave and say somethin' nice to him. You understand? When you talk to him we'll know he's still there.' The bold eyes were fixed on Wheeler like the eyes of a lidless rattler. 'Go do it, Mister Wheeler. I'll be watching an' you wouldn't want to try and warn a murderer anyway, would you?'

Art Wheeler's indecisiveness of moments earlier had been bent by the eyes and attitude of Uriah Kimball until he no longer was able to think for himself. And there was something else to influence him: he had for eleven years lived with the feeling that he was an alien in a place inhabited by people no white man ever really understood. He'd never felt secure among them even though he got along well with them. He had wondered many times what would happen if trouble came to the settlement; he was the only white man for many miles. If help arrived it would never do so in time. That sublimated fear made him an easy target for someone like the four Coloradans even though he had never thought trouble would come this way.

The stranger who had laughed with him a couple of hours earlier while drinking sarsparilla was a likable individual, but nothing compared with survival. Wheeler said, 'I got no use for murderers.'

Kimball hooked thumbs in his old worn

shellbelt and nodded at the storekeeper. 'Go over and look out there. Don't go outside, just look around.' There was nothing remaining of Kimball's earlier soft-spoken amiability.

Wheeler turned along the counter, emerged from behind it walking in the direction of the rear doorway. Behind him Kimball raised his voice slightly to the men over at the weapon counter. 'He's here. He's out back gettin' the bay horse shod. The storekeeper's goin' to signal us from the doorway if he's still back there. Charley, you go out front and slip around toward the back from the north. Junior, you go slip around from the south. Me'n Henry'll use the back door. Shoot the minute you see the son of a bitch.'

Two of the saddle-worn men left the building by the front door. The Navajo clerk's black eyes were motionless and glazed. He moved in jerks putting away the guns and closing the case.

The man named Henry turned to watch Wheeler at the back door, and without looking away sprayed tobacco juice on the floor. He was a young-old man; his face was lined and leached from exposure, his gaze was alert and fox-like. He could have been twenty-five or thirty-five.

Art unbarred the door, opened it softly and stepped into the opening peering slightly to his left with Uriah and Henry watching him like falcons.

Frank was putting silver coins into the open palm of the horse-shoer, caught movement from the corner of his eye and turned to gaze over where Wheeler was standing in the doorway his expression tight enough to stretch the skin over its bones. Frank dropped the last coin, the Indian said something and stooped to pick up his short length of railroad track, and Frank felt hair bristling at the nape of his neck. The storekeeper called over to him in a strained voice. 'Now you're fixed up, eh?'

The words rang with hollow friendliness. Frank stepped back, nearly colliding with the shoer, and a fluid silhouette sucked away from the edge of the building. The silent yell of warning in Frank's brain brought sudden fierce life to his nerves and muscles. He sprang toward the corral gate.

From the south where he had no reason to expect it someone fired at him and missed, but broke several stakes in the faggot gate. He dove past and landed in drying mud within the corral where his horse looked around in astonishment as Frank rolled to one side and drew as he was coming up to his knees.

Those palisaded upright flimsy faggots were so close together, held in place by the wire woven among them that it was nearly impossible to see inside or to see outside; this offered a measure of protection, but the pieces of dry wood were fragile and would not turn lead.

Frank crossed swiftly to the far side intending to break out over there when a man's bull-like voice yelled in anger. 'Gawddammit, you let him get away. *After him!*'

Nothing heavier than a cat could scale the faggot fence without becoming entangled in the wreckage its weight would cause so Frank kicked hard to break the lower lengths of wood. His horse was like a carving, motionless and staring; he had never seen his owner acting like a desperate trapped animal before.

The faggots broke cleanly; only the Lord knew how old that wood was. It snapped under each kick. He alternately aimed his kicks and looked over his shoulder. If one of them got up beside the crooked sticks and peered through Frank would be visible to him.

He did not wonder who they were; instinct told him. When the hole was barely large enough Frank looked for the last time toward the gate then dropped and hurled himself through the hole. His shirt tore, and a spiky tag-end raked his ribs drawing blood, but he was outside when he rolled and came up to his feet.

The stillness was almost suffocating. There was not a sound. To the left and right of the corral open ground trampled free of any kind of growth for generations stretched as far as the first residences. The one to the north was made of adobe and stood as square as a cube. The one to the south was like a large beehive and had a waterproof tarpaulin pegged down over its dome. The thing was made of mud-wattle and flat stones. A faint trickle of smoke rose from the smoke-hole in the roof.

He turned toward the beehive-house—called a hogan—because the corral ran in that direction with several sheds, probably storerooms, beyond to provide cover about half the distance, at least on the west side which was where the attack had originated. In all other directions it was open country.

Frank sprinted. Behind him a voice made harsh by wrath bellowed in loud English. 'Get around in back. *Find him! Kill him!*'

He reached the hogan, and without braking his charge hit the hide door-flap and was plunged into a smelly circular room so dark he could see nothing although he heard scuttling sounds as astonished Navajos sprang out of his way.

He sat up, dimly discerned two men, one very old and straggly, the other much younger, stalwart and lighter than most Indians, pressing against the back of the house. There was a young Navajo woman wearing a full, long skirt who jangled with bracelets and necklaces as she fluttered over to press against the younger buck.

Frank stood up, panting. The hogan needed

an airing. It smelled powerfully of cooked fat and human perspiration. Its inhabitants were staring at him without seeming to be breathing. He had nothing to say to them, even if he could have made himself understood, but he grabbed a Winchester saddlegun near the door-flap and checked it for loads. It was fully charged. This the Indians seemed to understand. They were pressing into the back wall so hard some crumbly bits of ancient earth fell from the domed ceiling. Frank was probably the epitome of evil to the Indians right at this moment; they would do absolutely nothing to turn his attention back to them.

Sound did not penetrate very well, the entire structure had been made of massive thicknesses of adobe, rocks and logs. Whatever entered including sound had to do so through the front opening, and it was not high enough for a grown person to squeeze through without hunching over, and now the old hide flap was back in place making the room even darker.

Frank used the end of the Winchester to ease the flap aside. A little light entered, but because the hogan did not face toward the morning sun there was no direct light. He propped the flap aside with someone's walking-stick, and stepped carefully to the south side in an effort to see up in the direction of the corral and the rear of the store.

CHAPTER TWELVE

SURVIVAL!

There was movement along the rear of the round corral. Frank knelt and raised the old carbine. He had got himself cornered, but there had been no alternative and at least they would have to smoke him out from the low doorway.

The movement faded. Whoever had been stalking from around in front of the corral may also have had one of those instinctive warnings. He did not cast another shadow.

Frank listened without really expecting to hear anything, and he twisted for a southward peek. Nothing. No sound, no movement, but they were coming, they were stalking him; this was the end of their month-long hunt for his blood.

He swung off sweat and glanced briefly toward the Indians. They could have been made of wood except for their eyes. As nearly as he could distinguish they did not have weapons. The old man with straggly grey hair and a beakish look to his thin old wrinkled countenance said something in a guttural whisper. Frank turned back to the opening. If the old buck was warning him it was not necessary.

The stillness stretched taut. If they knew he was in here they would come around on the blind side, which was in all directions except where the door-hole was. He watched, glanced at the rush and mud ceiling, decided it would not burn, and raised a soiled cuff to squeeze off more sweat.

He had no idea how they had found him but was sure they had not done it by tracking him.

There were no taunting shouts, no attempt to convince Frank he would be safe if he surrendered. The Kimballs had only one thing in mind; they would neither stop their efforts nor compromise.

He heard a horse walking, but faintly. If the ground had not been mushy after the rain he would have been able to guess the direction the horse was taking. But a walking horse did not come to him as a threat.

He had knelt so long his legs ached. He arose to flex them and looked around for a water-jug. There was an olla hanging over near the mud oven. He drank from it, replaced it and slipped back where he could see out.

There was a little scratching sound along the back of the hogan. The Indians reacted to it by sidling farther away. Frank twisted to look—and missed seeing a shadow move very rapidly across the door-hole, but when he turned back the old man hissed and pointed stiffly toward the doorway.

The old Indian's face, which resembled the rivulets carved in brown stone over a million years of storms, was alight with excitement. Frank looked out the door-hole as the old man seemed to be instructing him to do, but there was nothing to see. He ignored the old man, settled against packed earth and thought rationally. The scratching sound stopped, but began again after a few minutes, and this time the old buck raised his right hand, two fingers stiffly extended, and began to make a circular motion.

Someone outside in back was boring a hole through the wall!

Obviously Frank's enemies knew where he was hiding. He shook his head and turned to watching the ground beyond the doorway again. The odds were piling against him. The two bucks whispered back and forth briefly, the old man gesturing toward the carbine as he spoke. Frank raised an arm to catch their attention, gripped the Old Winchester in his fist and scowled. The Indians became silent.

He picked up stealthy sign on the blind side of the door-hole. It started and stopped, then started again. It was so faint if the door-flap had not been hanging aside he could not have detected it. He could not now circle around and come up on the opposite side in order to see out there, southward. He had to lie and wait.

If it was the intention of the man stalking him

against the mud wall from the south to shove a sixgun around without exposing himself and emptying it inside the room, he would have to expose his hand and part of his arm. Frank brought the Indian saddlegun down lower and waited.

The stalker stopped moving.

Behind, the boring was starting again. Frank ignored it because he had to. They were going to get him after all, it seemed. He cocked the old saddlegun, waiting for the gunhand and arm.

What came was not a gun nor even an exposed arm. Someone flattened against the thick wall perhaps a foot south of the door-hole, grunted and hurled something through the doorway. Pitch-smoke and oily flame filled the hogan within moments.

Frank used the Winchester to roll the firebrand into reach, grabbed the thing and flung it outside. The moment he did this someone fired from the north somewhere, the bullet struck an iron cooking-pot, broke it and sang off with a chilling sound.

Frank flattened, pushed the Winchester forward, strained to catch a sighting and got one. The shooter had been over near the rear of the trading-post. Frank tried to sight through oily black smoke out where the harmless firebrand was fiercely burning. He fired. The sound inside the hogan was deafening.

He had missed. The startled Coloradan sprang ahead and flew around a corner of the building.

Frank lowered the old gun, looked at it, looked at the Indians and bitterly said, 'What do you folks use these things for, prying up rocks?'

He got no reply. The firebrand had frightened the Indians, but the ricocheting bullet off their iron pot had dropped them to crouching positions along the rear wall.

Frank's anger was about half frustration. He was a good shot with either a saddlegun or a sixgun and at that distance he should have scored a hit. If he had to rely on this old Winchester he was worse off than ever.

Someone, probably the man his near miss had lent wings to, tried an angling shot into the hogan's interior. Where the slug struck alone, dust and dirt filled the air. Frank could not fire back without exposing himself because he could not see the Coloradan.

The old bronco craned around with cords standing out of his scrawny neck, then trilled and pointed. Maybe he could see the gouging tool beginning to come through the wall into the room but Frank could not. He nevertheless signalled with his sixgun for the old man to move clear, then steadied up his wrist and fired. Because sixguns made more noise than carbines, this time the deafening roar made

Frank's ears ring for a long time after the mud and stone and cloud of dust had begun to settle. His bullet had penetrated thick adobe exactly where the gouging had weakened it. Out back someone cried out. Inside no one could hear the frantic withdrawal of the borer, but since there was no further effort to make a loophole in the rear wall it was reasonable to assume that he had departed.

Frank methodically punched out the casing and plugged in a replacement as he waited. How long he could survive was moot. The Coloradans were absolutely determined. They would not ride away until he was dead. There was nothing to say to make them change their minds. When he had shot the other two, although he had known who the Kimball brothers were, he had not known how blindly dogged they could be even though he had suspected that they would come after him—but not for a solid month and not without even seeming to rest in their ride for vengeance.

He finished reloading and looking up in time to see a ball of greasy flame erupt near the back wall of the trading-post. It seemed to be huge, and before he could find something to fire at the fireball was hurled violently toward the door-hole.

This time it was not pitch-wood, it was coal oil. Coal oil fires did not respond to water. The fireball reached the doorway while losing momentum, but it had enough left to roll inside, except that Frank aimed at its centre and fired from less than ten feet away. Most of the oil-soaked balled-up cloth was punched violently back away from the door-hole where it broke, flinging scraps of furiously burning cloth in all directions. The part which was not hurled clear broke up and burned with oily smoke along the base and front of the hogan.

The smell was bad enough, but black smoke seemed to be sucked toward the door-hole. Frank swung his hat, but the smoke did not seem to diminish any. He dumped the hat on the back of his head and squeezed his eyes to keep the water from blurring vision, then inched ahead for what he assumed was to follow, and it did.

Two men began firing sixguns as they zigzagged toward the door-hole. They probably did not intend to enter, just to line up on both sides of the hole and empty their weapons into the hogan. That kind of attack would probably kill all four inhabitants.

Frank saw them running as wavery blears of unlikely man-shapes and settled his gun-fist against the ground, barrel tilted. When he fired the noise deafened him again, and a cloud of very dense smoke was roiled in the doorway.

He had killed a man without knowing it for moments, until the smoke rose and he could see the body in a wild sprawl with blood spreading from beneath it.

A great scream of wild fury filled the void of the gunshot echo. There was no sign of the other attacker who had run in behind the cover of black smoke. Frank dared not peek around the door-hole to see if he had got against the hogan out there.

He wiped his eyes, spat and pulled the old carbine up close at hand, then reloaded again as the stench and smoke began to die down.

The Indians were flat on the ground as far from Frank and the door-hole as they could get. Once he flung a look in their direction; both the young Indians were hiding their faces but the turkey-necked old man with the wildly streaming grey hair and shiny obsidian eyes had his mouth open in what was either a toothless grin or a grimace.

Over along the rear wall of the trading-post to the south where Frank could not see them, men opened up with Winchesters methodically and furiously firing into the hogan's thick mud wall.

At a range of something like forty yards it was not impossible a bullet might find a weak place in the old hard-baked mud and penetrate, but if one did, since the shooters were aiming at what would have been belt-buckle high if the people inside had been standing erect, no one would be injured because they were flat on the ground, and if they lowered their trajectory to that level the bullets would strike stone because the builders of this traditional Navajo house had not used adobe mud until they had made about four courses of flat stone completely around the hogan.

But none of the people inside felt invulnerable as the enraged Coloradans continued to fire. When one slide was shot empty the other guns continued to blaze away until the empty weapon had been reloaded.

To Frank it sounded like a full-scale battle. No one carried that much ammunition with them. In this case they did not have to, all they had to do was scream for Art Wheeler to throw them fresh cartons of bullets.

CHAPTER THIRTEEN

BLOOD!

The dead man was clearly visible once the coal-oil soaked rags burned down to little more than wisps of greasy smoke. He had not moved even a finger since he'd dropped. The blood from beneath him had ceased to flow and was turning to dark jelly where indentations in the drying mud contained it.

The ferocity of the fight was a testimony to how the Kimballs reacted when one of the clan was killed. No one had to tell Frank Walker that; they had been after him by night and day for a month over the previous killings. This time though, with their dead kinsman grotesquely sprawled only a short distance from the hogan door-hole plainly in their sight, the Kimball men seemed to discard caution in favour of an unalterable ferocity fed by rage. They shot up the front of the hogan first, then began concentrating on the door-hole.

Cooking-pots were shot off their hooks, the ash from the cooking circle was cascaded into the air making visibility deteriorate further; it had never been good inside the hogan, and once the woman cried out as a bullet shattered the hanging olla showering her with water.

A thick wooden box had the hasp shot off, the broken lock catapulted like shrapnel inside the room. Frank had no time to consider the damage nor did he look around at the people except for a brief moment when the woman had cried out. He did not see the sinewy old man with the unkempt hair peer through ash-dust at the broken box, then suddenly lunge inside it with claw-like fingers attached to a stringy arm. The old man fumbled, got up onto his knees to facilitate his frantic searching and abruptly reach deeply then sprang back with toothless gums exposed by a diabolical grin.

He turned and crawled rapidly around the wall until he was opposite Frank with the doorway between them. He raised up still widely and wetly grinning and pitched something across the opening.

Frank spared a second to glance down at the object which had landed beside him. The old man was on his haunches watching, black eyes dazzling bright through squeezed-up flesh from his wild grin.

Frank reached, lifted a tube with wax on it and stared. An eight-inch braided black fuse extended from the upper end of the stick of dynamite he was holding. He looked at the old man, who made wild gestures and keened a series of shrill indistinguishable words which overrode the gunfire noise.

Frank reconsidered the reddish tube, leaned slightly, as far as he dared, and risked a look outside. They were emptying their guns from over along the back-wall of the trading post, but he could not see them without exposing more of himself.

He knew roughly where they were and put down his sixgun, shot the old maniac across the doorway from him another stare, then fished for his matches.

The old man's wet smile fairly split his face. He was sitting back on his haunches with both hands on his upper legs, watching everything Frank did with drooling fascination.

When the match ignited the fuse the old man began to make frantic throwing motions. Frank ignored him and watched the fuse burn. The old man's grin congealed, his ferret-like eyes widened with slow horror as Frank continued to hold the dynamite stick. When there was no more than about three inches of fuse still burning, Frank leaned forward, risking being shot, and with a high overhand fling which made him grunt from the powerful effort hurled the red tube in a high tumbling arc, then as he was pulling back something like a branding iron seared with white-hot heat below his upflung arm and his left side and he went sideways unable to lower the arm soon enough to catch himself.

He had one moment to feel sticky wetness beneath his torn shirt then the world blew apart with an ear-splitting sound accompanied by shock waves that beat past the door-hole to fill the room.

The blinding orange-white light lasted no more than a couple of seconds. When it died the interior of the hogan seemed darker than it had been before.

Sounds continued to come after the dynamite's echo began to sound distant and more like a rolling series of deep growls.

Frank put his right hand under his left arm against the sticky flesh and pulled it up close to his face. Unlike the Navajo woman who had been drenched with water. Frank's hand was covered with something equally as wet, but stickier and red in colour.

He twisted as much as possible to examine the wound. There was not enough light left in the dust-laden air, but he began to feel stinging pain.

He probed the wound, determining its extent by feel alone. The bullet had struck on a downward course tearing most of what was left of his ragged, filthy shirt. It had made a ragged flesh-wound which was pumping blood, but he found no broken ribs, so if he could staunch the flow of blood he thought he would probably survive.

Finally, all the noise ceased. There was dust hanging all along the rear of the trading-post. Mingled with its musty scent was an aroma which could have been made by gunpowder, except that it wasn't.

The old man was inching over for a peek out the door-hole. Frank snapped at him. 'Keep back!' Even if the old Indian could have understood he would not have obeyed.

The younger Indians called quickly in their own language, but the old man ignored them too. He was like a target in a shooting gallery for anyone out there to fire at, then began leaning back away from the doorway again, grinning like a crazy person. He faced half around and rolled a flow of crowing words to the younger Indians and ended up by slapping his thigh with considerable force, then he arose and walked back where they were easing up into a sitting posture and stood beating his chest and haranguing them.

The woman saw Frank's condition and approached him. She knelt without looking into his face, leaned close to examine the gory-looking injury, then arose and went over among the broken cooking utensils to select items from a wooden crate which was dowelled to the wall close to the shattered olla.

When she returned she said something in her native language, still without looking Frank in the face, and when this elicited no response she tried Spanish, and without waiting for an answer she unfolded cotton cloth and leaned to cleanse the injury, which hurt like hell before she began and hurt much more afterwards.

She fashioned a wide body bandage, but first lathered the injury with sheep-grease, the Navajo panacea for external injuries—not theirs alone; people all over the world had been using lanolin as a healant for thousands of years.

Frank knelt leaning back while she worked on him. There was not a sound beyond the hogan, but he was not convinced that his blindly thrown dynamite stick had eliminated the Kimballs. He thought it had probably stunned, perhaps even awed them, and it had certainly stopped their savage gunfire-attack, but he had the sixgun in his hand again. The Kimballs were a blind-stubborn and hard-bitten crew.

There was silence for a very long time. Meanwhile the woman completed her bandaging and returned again to the rear of the hogan where the old man and the younger man were sitting, the old man grinning like a monkey, the young man drifting shocked glances around his devastated home.

The old man got to his feet to dig through an untidy assortment of ancient horsehair riding equipment, moth-eaten blankets and soiled clothing. When he turned toward Frank he was holding a large medicine bottle. He pulled it open and held it out.

Frank sniffed. The aroma was rather like a combination between ether and whisky. He regarded the old man dubiously. From back in the settling dust and gloom the young Indian said, '*Pulque*,' as though he expected the white man to understand. Frank knew; he had first heard of *pulque* from the wounded outlaw back at the rancheria. He sniffed again. The old Navajo laughed, took back the bottle, threw his head and swallowed several times then handed it back to Frank, grinning from ear to ear.

Frank warily tasted the liquor; it was the worst beverage he had ever tasted in his life. He firmly handed the bottle back and scowled as he shook his head. If the old buck's feelings were hurt it did not affect his wide grin as he turned away.

A sudden unsteady call rang out from the

direction of the trading-post. Frank did not reply. There was a long interval, then the call was repeated, this time with words which were distinguishable. Also, Frank thought he knew the voice. He answered without showing himself.

'What do you want, Wheeler?'

'Mister Chambers? Are you all right?'

'What in hell does that have to do with the Kimballs?' Frank called back.

'Two of them are dead. One of 'em we got to find all the pieces yet.'

'Too bad,' Frank called back. 'What do you want?'

'The other two—the oldest one and another feller—I got them in chains.'

Frank's side felt like it was on fire despite the soothing properties of sheep-oil. He shifted around in order to have something to lean against before speaking again. Each time he took down a big breath and strained to shout, the pain intensified in his side. 'You want me to come out, is that it?'

Wheeler's reply was quick. 'Yes. It's safe. Is anyone hurt in there?'

Frank did not answer the second part of the call. After a moment of thought he said, 'Fetch the pair you got in chains out where I can see them.'

Wheeler did not respond. In fact, Frank, who'd had suspicions, was beginning to think

Wheeler for some reason had been trying to lure him out of the hogan into plain sight. He and the Indians looked at one another.

'Mister Chambers? Look outside.'

Frank did not move until the old Navajo leaned so far to his left he seemed about to topple over. He could see the area in front of the hogan and chirped something to the younger Indians. The buck spoke in English when he said, 'Two white men tied with chains on the arms. No guns. No hats. The trader is behind them.'

Frank still did not move. 'Does the trader have a gun?'

'A shotgun,' the Indian replied.

Frank sighed, then pulled down another deep and painful breath before calling out. 'Wheeler, put that shotgun down and herd those two fellers a little closer to the hogan, then turn their backs to me.'

The young Indian, probably emboldened by what the old man had done first, leaned, then arose and moved stealthily closer to the door-hole by keeping well to one side of it. He leaned, looked, and said, 'He put down the shotgun. The other men have their backs to us. He is making them walk backwards.'

Frank picked up the useless Winchester with the bent barrel, and using it for a walking-aid raised and uncocked his sixgun with the other hand, and hesitated long enough to look at the

Indians. They were crowding in closer to the door, exposing themselves as they did so.

Frank looked at the woman. At first she turned quickly away, then she turned back to meet his gaze as he said, 'I'm sorry about all this. If they have any money I'll get it for you.'

She looked at the young buck, but he did not interpret at once, he simply stood gazing at the nearly shirtless, blood-spattered white man with the haggard face and sunken eyes.

Frank smiled. 'Tell her I owe her whatever she wants for patching me up. Go ahead, tell her.'

The Indian spoke to his wife. She listened, then turned slightly aside, and her husband nodded to Frank. 'All her pots are broken.'

Frank hitched around leaning on the old carbine. The moment he appeared in the door-hole Wheeler's jaw dropped and his eyes grew round.

Frank had to bend to leave the hogan. The pain this caused made his breath catch. Even after he straightened up in bright sunshine, the pain hung on.

Wheeler sounded awed when he said, 'You look bad hurt, Mister Chambers.'

Frank walked around in front of the Kimballs. He recognized the oldest one and the youngest one. They looked icily at him. Both men had chains wrapped and locked around their arms in front. They were sweaty, filthy and rumpled. He pointed his uncocked sixgun at the greying man. 'You're Uriah. Who is this man?'

Uriah's jaw muscles rippled from the pressure of locked jaw. Raw fury shone from his eyes and he did not answer. Frank cocked the sixgun, looking the eldest Kimball directly in the eye.

The other prisoner quickly spoke up. 'I'm Junior. Youngest of the six of us Kimball brothers.'

Frank was still looking directly at the older man and did not acknowledge that he had heard. He tipped up the barrel. Wheeler's features seemed to tighten. His eyes bulged in horror. 'Don't,' he exclaimed shakily. 'It's murder, Mister Chambers.'

Frank turned the gun slowly in Wheeler's direction. 'How did they get all that ammunition; you gave it to them?'

'No. No sir, Mister Chambers, I swear to gawd. They came inside and filled their shirts with cartons of bullets. I couldn't do anything.'

Frank's gunbarrel did not waver. 'How did you manage to use the shotgun, then, Mister Wheeler?'

'The explosion—it hit right close to the feller who was blown up. It tore chunks of adobe and rocks from the back of the store. The feller with the grey hair caught one as big as a melon square on top of his head. That other one tried to run and got knocked flat, stunned I expect. I got my twelve-gauge and some chain before they come around. Mister Chambers, I—'

'My name is Frank Walker, not Chambers,' Frank said, eyeing the trader. 'How did they find out I was here?'

'Well—I expect they saw your horse or—'

'You mealy-souled miserable bastard,' Uriah Kimball exclaimed. 'You told us he was here. Go ahead, tell him the rest of it—you even told us where he was an' what he was doing!'

Frank turned slowly away from the white-faced trader to stare at Uriah Kimball. 'I guess you'll never quit, will you? As long as you can breathe you'll keep huntin' me down.'

The finger inside the trigger-guard began to gradually curl with the trigger inside it. The trader looked as though he would faint, but Uriah Kimball held Frank's eyes with a venomous glare. 'Shoot,' he said. 'You killed two of my brothers up in Colorado without givin' them a chance.'

Frank said, 'You're a damned liar and you know it. They came to town to ambush me between them because I saw the six of you rebranding stolen cattle back in that big mountain meadow. I didn't have any choice but to shoot first and fastest. As for that dead man lying yonder and the feller who got blown up—it was you who's been pushing for this ever since you taken up my trail. Kimball, I'm going to kill you!'

The rawboned, greying older man with the expression of a savage glared back and thundered his reply. 'Do it! Damn you, pull that trigger!'

The ashen much younger man in chains at his side cried out in a wild voice directed toward Frank. 'No! Don't do it for gawd's sake. It wasn't him!' He jerked his head to indicate the dead man face down near by. 'It was him and Henry. They worked it up with my two brothers you shot. They sent them down to ambush you. Uriah didn't know anything about it.'

The big greying man turned slowly to stare. Junior Kimball had wet eyes and an ugly twist to his mouth as he said, 'That's the truth, Uriah. They made me swear never to tell you they sent Greg and Joe after Walker. They was afraid of what you'd do if you knew they got 'em killed.' For a moment the younger man panted for breath, then faced away from his remaining brother and spoke more calmly. 'Henry's yonder. Charley got blown up. That's enough, Uriah.' He looked at Frank. 'It wasn't him; he figured you'd caught them in town and shot them without warning. I wanted to say something—wanted to for a month while we was after you, only it looked like you was going to get clear and I hoped to gawd you would.'

Frank's side was burning with a steady pain.

He looked around, saw the rear-door steps of the trading-post and went to sit down with the cocked Colt hanging between his knees. He had gone just about as far as he could go.

Uriah Kimball had not moved nor taken his eyes off his younger brother. He seemed to age even as Frank looked at him.

Art Wheeler walked over to also sit down, but he did not sit near Frank Walker, he righted a slab-wounded keg and sat on that near a wide, crumbly crack in the rear wall of his building. Frank spoke to him without looking around or raising his voice.

'Fetch me some water, Mister Wheeler.'

The trader arose and departed quickly, leaving Frank and the Kimballs looking at one another. He knew the kind of man Uriah was; he had known many like him. Wild horses would be unable to tear words out of him about his terrible and fatal mistake.

He calmly said, 'You son of a bitch, Kimball.'

The greying man did not respond. He was not actually looking at Frank, he was looking at something invisible to everyone else about six inches above Frank's head.

CHAPTER FOURTEEN

END OF THE TRAIL

Art Wheeler herded his prisoners around in front and across the road to the adobe jailhouse and locked them into a cell without removing their chains. He returned to his store where Frank was being worked over by his clerk and another Indian, a greying, gaunt man with mahogany-coloured hide and a headband.

When Wheeler entered and saw the exposed wound, he swallowed and avoided Frank's gaze as he scuttled behind a counter and emerged moments later with a pony of malt whisky which he handed to Frank.

Frank held the bottle and looked at the trader. 'Fetch their outfits in here,' he said, and did not raise the bottle until Wheeler had hurried off to obey. Then he drank. It was good whisky. It did not ameliorate the pain where that gaunt man was trimming off ragged skin, but it helped clear Frank's mind.

When Wheeler returned grunting under the weight of the saddles and dumped them in front of Frank he was given another order. 'Go clean out the pockets of those bastards you locked up and bring that stuff over here too. Where is that Indian constable you said lived here?'

Wheeler did not answer, his clerk, the young man with the brown-paper sleeve-protectors did. 'He rode away before those other white men rode in.' The clerk's black eyes lifted briefly to meet Frank Walker's gaze, and he shrugged, lowered his eyes and continued to help the Navajo healer.

Frank snarled at Wheeler. 'Go clean out their pockets. What're you waiting for?'

Again Wheeler hastened away. After he was gone Frank looked down to watch the rebandaging, had another swallow of the malt whisky, and told the clerk to detach saddlebags from the nearby saddles and bring them to him.

The gaunt Indian seemed detached from everything happening around him as he trimmed flesh, cleaned the wound, then pulled the two torn parts together, and with deft fingers made a series of closures before smearing sheep-grease over the freshly dressed wound and starting the bandaging. He looked briefly annoyed when Frank picked up one of the saddlebags to unbuckle it and fish inside, but the Indian said nothing.

His annoyance was replaced by surprise when Frank fished forth a fistful of greenbacks, and when Art Wheeler returned with the things he had been sent to the jailhouse for he stopped stone-still.

Frank looked up at Wheeler. 'Fetch me a big paper bag to hold this stuff.'

Wheeler put down the things he had brought from the jailhouse and went behind a counter. The gaunt Navajo straightened up, drying his fingers on a scrap of gingham cloth. He was more interested in his handiwork than he was in the crushed and crumbled greenbacks Frank systematically stuffed into the paper sack, but neither of the other onlookers were; they stared. What Frank finally got stuffed into the bag was an awful lot of money. More than the store-clerk had ever seen at one time, and perhaps more than his employer Art Wheeler had seen in one lump in a long while.

Frank put the paper sack at his feet and told the store-clerk to sift through the things his employer had brought from the jailhouse and pick out all the money.

Wheeler looked on with interest but no comprehension until the clerk held up both hands with money in them, and Frank said, 'Take it around to those folks who own that hogan that got all shot up and give it to them.'

The clerk's gaze wavered from Frank to the money and over to his employer. Frank pointed a rigid finger. 'All of it. You understand? Every damned cent of it. Get out of here!'

The young Indian departed.

Wheeler smiled at Frank, whose colour was high and whose strength seemed to have been revived by the malt whisky. 'This In'ian is the best healer in the countryside. You'll be good as new before you know it.'

Frank eyed the gaunt Indian, fished for some silver cartwheels and held them forth. The Indian continued to dry his hands for a moment while studying the money being offered. Eventually he pocketed the gingham cloth and selected two of the silver dollars, nodded solemnly at Frank and walked out of the store.

Frank watched him depart with a puzzled look until the trader explained. 'He took two because he needs a new pair of rowels for his spurs. That's what they make 'em out of.'

Frank considered the other three cartwheels, then shrugged and pocketed them. These damned people didn't even live in the same world, let alone the same century, as other people.

Wheeler said, 'You're lookin' better. I got a little phial of laudanum.'

Frank had been sitting in an armless old chair during the bandaging. Being without arms it made turning toward the trader easier. He did not say anything, he just sat looking at the trader.

Wheeler reddened. 'What else could I do? I know their type and there was four of 'em. They was here for blood. I wasn't carrying a weapon. Mister Chambers—uh—Mister Walker what else could I have done?'

Frank continued to look at the trader in silence for a while before he answered. 'Being you—nothing. Here, take the bottle.' As Wheeler leaned to extend an arm Frank said, 'Their backs were to you while they fired from near the rear-wall of this building, and you were in the store with ammunition and guns—that shotgun at least. Naw, you couldn't have done anything. Is my horse all right?'

Wheeler fled to find out, and the young Indian came in wearing a bemused smile. 'They didn't want to take it,' he said. 'They said you were a very brave man. They sent you this.' He held out his hand. Frank accepted the pair of identical circular beaded hair-braid decorations. He looked up. 'You left the money—all of it?'

'Yes. Do you know how much there was?'

'I don't care how much there was as long as it was enough.'

'It was more than they could count. It was two hundred dollars.'

Frank studied the intricate beadwork of the circular objects in his hand. Eventually he leaned back and regarded the young Indian. 'You speak pretty fair English.'

'I'm not a full-blood. I grew up in Taos; the town not the pueblo.' The clerk's eyes brightened a little. 'I can't speak Navajo very good.' He grinned ruefully, and Frank grinned back.

'You work for a sorry son of a bitch,' Frank said, still smiling at the younger man. 'Don't be like him.' He saw flashing movement near the sunlighted front doorway and looked past. The toothless old Navajo with long, straggly and unkempt hair was hovering out there as though afraid to enter. He was wearing holed moccasins and the same soiled britches and patched shirt he had been wearing in the hogan during the fight. He was also grinning from ear to ear.

Frank laughed and used his right arm to motion the old man inside. The clerk turned, then turned back toward Frank and said in English, 'Mister Wheeler don't let him in. He steals.'

Frank acted deaf. When the old man was close Frank pushed out his hand and said, 'Shake, partner.' The old man knew no English, but under these circumstances he did not have to. He pumped Frank's hand and chortled in delight. He even cast a challenging glance at the store-clerk.

Frank freed his hand and spoke in English again. 'Lay him out some new pants and a couple of new shirts; maybe some stockings if he uses 'em, and find some bright red bandanas.' He paused, eyeing the young Indian. 'An' you smile.'

The young man smiled and was still smiling when he turned toward the shelves, but it was a strain.

Wheeler returned to report that the mule-nosed bay horse was fine and that he had pitched him an extra bait of hay—free of charge—and saw the toothless old bony relic of earlier times standing there in his filthy clothing grinning from ear to ear. He glared.

Frank pointed a finger. 'Mister Wheeler, this oldtimer is my particular friend; he's more of a man in five minutes than you are all day. Someday I'm goin' to come ridin' back through here. I don't want to hear that you wouldn't let him in your store.'

Wheeler's face reddened. 'He steals. I've known him since I first came here, an' I used to let him come into the store, but the old devil liked to stole me blind.'

Frank grinned at the old Navajo and made a motion for him to go over where the clerk was laying out his new clothing. As soon as he was gone Frank said, 'Mister Wheeler, how much do you suppose an old man could steal off you over, say, five, six years?'

The trader scowled. 'I've got no idea. Lots of 'em steal, but not like that old man; I've been standin' right there watching him, an' when he grins and walks out something's missing. I've never caught him red-handed. Damnedest thing you ever saw.'

'How much, Mister Wheeler?'

'Well—'

Frank reached down into the stuffed paper bag and brought out a greenback of fairly large denomination. 'This much?'

Wheeler eyed the money. 'Did you say five or

six years?'

Frank nodded. 'How old do they live to be?'

Wheeler continued to eye the money. 'I expect that'd cover all he'll steal in five or six years, Mister Chambers.'

Wheeler accepted the money and looked over where his clerk was laughing at the old man's child-like joy over his new wardrobe, then Wheeler sighed, pocketed the money and faced Frank to say something when the distinct ring of shod hooves out in the roadway reached every person inside the store.

Wheeler went to peer out, and pulled back as though he had been stung, whirled and hurried back inside to say, 'Seven riders—white men.' He seemed close to panic. 'Armed—oh my gawd!'

Frank arose carefully to walk ahead. He was shirtless, bandaged, sunken-eyed, unshaven with stiff dark blood on his trousers. He looked like the sole survivor of a massacre when he stepped out into the sunlight, and the riders in the roadway saw him and halted to stare.

He nodded gravely to them. 'Morning, Mister Duryea,' he drawled. 'If you'd step inside I think I got something that belongs to the folks at Bent's Crossing.'

Duryea said nothing until one of his companions swung off to lead his horse to the trading-post tie-rack and wag his head at Frank Walker. 'You look like you been through a meat-grinder,' he said.

Duryea finally reined over and dismounted. He was evidently a man whose surprises came and went fast. As he looped reins and studied Frank Walker he said, 'Mister Chambers,' in a voice that implied doubt about the name and the man he was staring at.

Frank ignored the inflection and asked about the outlaw he had known as John Smith. This was an area where none of the seven horsemen were reticent. 'Dead,' stated a husky short man with a wide space between his two upper front teeth which facilitated aiming when he spat tobacco juice.

Duryea leaned on the rack studying Frank Walker. 'Yeah, he got himself killed,' Duryea stated almost indifferently. 'Those fellers who were looking for that Walker-feller killed him.'

Frank returned the stare. 'And?'

'And—they made off with his saddlebag, Mister Chambers—and—some In'ians drivin' sheep met 'em this morning real early. They told us those fellers headed for Blue House.' Duryea straightened up and lifted his hat to mop at sweat, still eyeing Frank. In an almost mocking voice he said, 'You haven't seen 'em by any chance, have you?'

Frank had never been very warmly attracted to the man he was facing. 'Yeah, I've seen them,' he replied, and jutted his chin in the direction of the adobe jailhouse. 'Two are over there locked up. One is lyin' dead out back, and the fourth one—I guess you and the post-trader in the store behind me can find pieces of him here and there.' Frank gave Duryea look for look. 'Come inside,' he said, and waited for the other man to start moving before he turned he lead the way.

All of the men from Bent's Crossing crowded into the trading-post. They could not avoid seeing the torn, bloody shirt on the floor near that armless chair where Frank had been sitting, nor the looks on the faces of the people over along one of the counters, including the broadly grinning old unkempt Navajo buck with the ropy long grey hair.

Frank picked up the paper sack and handed it to Duryea. 'I didn't count it. But if they didn't get a chance to spend it before they got down here it ought to be there.' As Duryea accepted the sack and looked inside it Frank also said, 'Except for one fifty-dollar greenback. I appropriated that.'

He eased down in the armless chair and shoved out his legs, gazing at the riders. Two of them strolled toward the sagging-open rear door and stood in the opening. Two other men were watching the two Indians, the very old one and the younger one. The clerk was trying to make all the clothing balance atop the old man's arms.

Art Wheeler came from behind his counter to

introduce himself to the riders from Bent's Crossing. They acknowledged his name with nods, only Duryea spoke to Wheeler. 'What in the hell happened here?'

Wheeler's tongue made a rapid circuit of his lips, and he glanced nervously at Frank before replying. 'Those four fellers who was after this feller—they started a fight.'

Duryea interrupted. 'After this feller; you mean Mister Chambers here?'

Art Wheeler's eyes jumped to Frank and back to Duryea. He cleared his throat, then said, 'Well—I don't really know what it was all about.'

Frank spoke up. 'My name is Frank Walker, not Burt Chambers. I think they told you the rest of it when you met them back up yonder—before they tried to run off with your money.'

A grinning horseman said, 'I told you, Hank. I told you this here feller was Walker.'

Duryea turned sharply. 'You want a medal for bein' right once in your life?'

The grinning man said no more, but his expression of self-satisfaction lingered.

Duryea looked into the brown paper bag again, then over at Frank. Before he could say anything Frank spoke up. 'Sometimes a man guesses right and sometimes he don't. You thought the Kimballs would bring back whatever they found on John Smith. You guessed wrong. You came after them figurin' they might be down here finishing me off like they did John Smith. Wrong again. And now you got your damned money back so you got one more guess. You want to guess whether I'm an outlaw or not? You want to try takin' me back to Bent's Crossing with you?'

The listening riders seemed bemused as they regarded Hank Duryea. They were neither lawmen nor manhunters; like Duryea they had ridden long and hard to retrieve the stolen money, and hopefully to settle with the bandit who had shot up their town to steal it.

Duryea looked into the bag again before saying, 'I know all that crap the Kimballs told us about you, Mister Walker. An' I know something else: you could have got away with this money after you cleaned those bastards out.' Duryea showed a barely discernible harsh smile. 'I don't care what you are, friend. We're not lawmen. We just wanted this money back and we're obliged for you getting it for us.'

Duryea turned toward the trader. 'You got any whisky?' he asked.

Wheeler made a deprecating gesture. 'This is an In'ian reservation and no one is allowed to—'

'I know that as well as you do,' snapped Hank Duryea. 'I asked—do you have any?'

Wheeler turned woodenly aside to retrieve the bottle he had brought to Frank. The two men in the rear doorway called back into the room. 'Hank—come look out here. There's been a gawdamned war. You never seen anythin' like it.'

Duryea remained rooted even though the other riders pushed toward the rear doorway. Duryea had three hearty swallows from Art Wheeler's illegal bottle, then blew out a big breath and said, 'How bad hurt are you?' to Frank, adding a little more. 'We got a good doctor over in Bent's Crossing. He used to do doctoring in the cavalry; a little rough but he knows his business. You'd be right welcome to ride back with us.'

Frank declined the offer with a small smile at Duryea. 'I'll be fit to ride in a few days. Thanks all the same, but all I want is to get as far from this country as a man can ride, then maybe find a place with trees and grass and maybe a creek running through where a man could make a camp—and not do a damned thing but maybe fish and hunt a little until the cows come home.'

Hank Duryea seemed to understand, at least he bobbed his head before heading for the back door where his riders had crowded out into the area behind the store.

Art Wheeler balanced between staying and going, decided to go and hurried after the seven men from Bent's Crossing. Frank and the two Indians remained in the store. The old man shuffled over drooling like a two-year-old. He made some kind of disconnected speech, then scuttled out of the store.

The young Navajo leaned atop the counter watching. When the old man had disappeared he said, 'I can tell you what he said if you want me to.'

They looked at each other. The Indian shrugged. 'He said only an idiot holds a stick of dynamite in his hand until the fuse is burning his fingers. You aren't going to live to be as old as he is, but he thanks you for the stuff you got for him.'

Frank laughed. The young Navajo grinned. 'You want a bath?' he asked, surprising Frank with the suggestion. The Indian pointed. 'Outside, then walk south. You'll see an old sweat-house. Behind it is a little creek. Wait. You need clean pants and shirt.'

He got them from the shelves. He was good at estimating sizes; he had to be because no Navajo ever had any idea what any of his sizes were—by white-man rules. As Frank arose to accept the clothing and a bar of tan lye soap he said, 'How much are the clothes?'

The clerk looked him squarely in the eye and said, 'I don't know and it don't matter anyway; you are right about Mister Wheeler, I don't want to be like him. I'll look after your horse. When you come back I'll make a food bundle for you. Don't get the bandage wet.'

Frank left the store and saw no Indians until he was down near the spindly little creek. There were two naked men and three naked women also bathing. When he stopped the men gestured for him to come and bathe.

He smiled at them and spent a full ten minutes arranging his new clothing on the ground. When he finished doing that they were still there. He sat down to kick off his boots and very methodically unbuckle and roll his gunbelt. They ignored him and talked among themselves. Clearly they were not going to finish bathing and depart.

He took longer removing his britches and socks than he ever had before in his life, and they went right ahead bathing. The men looked over, evidently intrigued by the length of time white men required to strip down for bathing.

Frank grinned feebly at them. Only one could—or at least would—speak English. He called over to Frank. 'Water clean. Warm too. Plenty room.'

Frank stood up in his underdrawers and began walking toward the creek. All five Indians straightened up to watch as he smiled and nodded and walked down into the creek in his drawers. They were transfixed as he leaned to lather with the lye soap. One of the women said something which elicited a response from the men.

Frank washed very carefully to avoid soaking his body bandage. The Navajo who knew English said, 'White man do bath and laundry together. Indian do them separately.'

All the Indians broke into laughter, and Frank got as red as a beet.

Photoset, printed and bound in Great Britain by
REDWOOD PRESS LIMITED, Melksham, Wiltshire